"I don't *need* you, Ryan. I'm willing to put up with you, that's all!"

"Oh, I think there's more to it than that, Nina. Much, much more...."

The trailing tip of thumb brushed the corner of her mouth, which parted in alarm.

When had he moved so close? "Don't touch me!"

"Why not?" His voice dropped to a bittersweet tenderness. "What are you so afraid of? What will happen if I do?"

"Nothing will happen!"

"All right. I won't—" he turned back to the house "—for now." He gave her a smoldering smile over his shoulder. "But we both know that I don't have to *touch* you for you to be *touched* by me, don't we...Nina, darling?"

Susan Napier

SECRET SEDUCTION

Amnesia

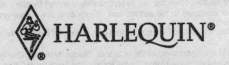

TORONTO • NEW YORK • LONDON
AMSTERDAM • PARIS • SYDNEY • HAMBURG
STOCKHOLM • ATHENS • TOKYO • MILAN • MADRID
PRAGUE • WARSAW • BUDAPEST • AUCKLAND

ISBN 0-373-12135-0

SECRET SEDUCTION

First North American Publication 2000.

Copyright © 2000 by Susan Napier.

CHAPTER ONE

ANOTHER salt-laden blast of wind funnelled past the low cliffs at the entrance of the bay and howled across the seething waves to dash itself against the ragged row of houses along the beachfront. In the back room of her rented cottage Nina Dowling flinched as the windows rattled violently in their sun-warped frames and the woodwork creaked and groaned in protest at the assault.

Hunching protectively over her desktop drawing board, she dipped her brush into the narrow-mouthed water jar at her elbow and meticulously reshaped the sable bristles, trying to block out her awareness of the growing tumult outside by concentrating on the intricate task at hand.

So what if she had just heard the radio weather bulletin issue an overnight gale warning for the Hauraki Gulf? Despite its ramshackle appearance, this sturdy bungalow had weathered more than fifty years of winter storms. And, anyway, Shearwater Island was in the southern reaches of the gulf, less exposed to the full force of the storms that regularly blew in from the Pacific Ocean than many of the other hundred or so islands that were scattered off the coast of Auckland.

A few minutes later, Nina gave up pretending that she was going to get any more work done. The ominous crack of approaching thunder was the last straw. Trying to etch the delicate path of a minute leaf vein with the moistened edge of her chisel-shaped brush tip was impossible when her nerves were braced against the next assault of nature. She pursed her ripe mouth as she surveyed what she had just done, her sea-green eyes narrowed with dissatisfaction,

her silky dark brows drawn together in a rippling frown.
Instead of abrading away the wash of green pigment to
expose a hair-thin line of white paper, the nervous jerks of
her clenched fingers were in danger of creating a major new
vein at the margin of the leaf.

Such botanical incorrectness would give George palpi-
tations! she thought ruefully as she set aside the unfinished
illustration and replaced the labelled pot containing the
original plant specimen on the crowded shelf by the window. While Nina freely employed a great deal of artistic
licence in her own paintings, the bread-and-butter commissions she executed for the local botanist demanded strict
biological accuracy. It was exacting work but Nina enjoyed
the challenge, and the flat fee that George paid her for each
completed watercolour was sufficient to support her in very
modest style.

Fortunately, there were few temptations to frivolous
spending on Shearwater Island. Most of the islanders were
laid-back alternative lifestylers, eccentric loners, or descen-
dants of original owners who either commuted to Auckland
to work or merely used their properties during weekends
and holidays.

Part of the island was a nature and marine reserve, and
the locals jealously guarded their relatively unspoiled environment by enduring rudimentary public services and
supporting by-laws that precluded commercial develop-
ment. That meant there were no chic beach cafés or hotels,
or well-serviced moorings for glitzy yachts on Shearwater
Island, no flash millionaires' mansions or noisy helipads.

The only store, at the wooden ferry jetty on the other
side of the island from Puriri Bay, stocked little more than
the basic necessities of life—except during the summer
months, when the resident population of a few hundred was
swollen by holiday-makers, visiting boaties who dropped

anchor in the deepwater bays and daytrippers who made the hour-and-a-half ferry ride from Auckland.

In the nine months that she had lived on the island, Nina had been pleased to discover that there was nothing that she couldn't buy, barter, mail-order or stoically go without.

Another shuddering gust of wind buffeted the house on its foundations as Nina cleaned her brushes with the speed and efficiency of long practise and covered her palette of watercolours with a damp cloth to prevent the shallow pans from drying out overnight. She carried the squat jars of stained water into the kitchen to rinse them out for the next day, flicking off the fluorescent lights in the cramped studio. Usually she preferred using the natural light from the sloping skylight and small, southerly facing window for her studio-based paintings, but the dense cloud cover had made artificial illumination necessary for most of the day.

Leaving her clean jars draining upside down on the bench, Nina hurried through the sprawling, three-bedroom cottage, making sure that all the external door and window latches were secure, and checking that there was nothing loose outside that high winds might turn into a potential missile.

In the last big storm, Ray Stewart, who lived in the sun-bleached weatherboard house next door, had almost been skewered in his rocking chair by an unsecured water-ski that had blown off someone's deck and cartwheeled along the wide strip of interconnecting front yards to spear through his window. The grizzled old man, who also happened to be Nina's landlord, had taken his near impalement in his stride, more angry at his neighbour's carelessness than frightened by his brush with mortality, but to Nina it had been a graphic warning of the awesome power of nature.

Now, standing in her living room, looking out at the deserted, wind-scoured beach, she wrapped her arms around her waist in an unconsciously self-protective gesture. The sliding glass door, misted with salt and sand, framed a panoramic view of the tempest. Along the grassy public foreshore, the huge, gnarled puriri trees that gave the bay its name were writhing, their twisted limbs semaphoring the rising strength of the wind, the thick, evergreen foliage tossing in sympathy with the storm-whipped sea.

Spray was thick in the swirling air and even the hardiest of seabirds, the squalling gulls, had taken cover. The tide was nearly full in, the greedy waves chewing more than halfway up the wide curve of sloping sand towards the low bank on which the puriri trees perched, their venerable roots knitted deep into the sandy clay.

Farther out, the deep swells pushing in from the gulf boomed onto the rocks at the base of the cliffs, exploding upwards in sheets of ghostly white foam that instantly dissolved into the jagged cliff face. Within the semicircle of the bay itself, the murky sea was a frenzy of whitecaps, the few boats still anchored there pitching and rolling as they strained at their moorings. Clumps of dirty white foam broke away from the building crest at the high-water line and swirled up onto the back of the beach, rolling and tumbling over moisture-darkened soft sand still pockmarked from earlier showers.

Although sunset was officially still hours away, it was already almost dark outside, the dense black clouds continuing to sweep in from the north-east, bringing with them forked flashes of lightning and a thick band of rain that blurred the gap between turbulent sky and tumultuous sea until they were indistinguishable from each other in the intensifying gloom.

The artist in Nina revelled in the visual drama of the scene. It was beautiful, wild...dangerous....

A cool frisson shivered up her spine and Nina hugged herself more tightly, glad that she had earlier lit the fire in the big stone hearth that dominated the open-plan living area. The temperature had been dropping all day, and even in her red polar-fleece sweatshirt, black jeans and sheepskin boots, she had shivered at the penetrating chill in the damp air when she slipped out to fetch a few armfuls of dry driftwood from the stack under the broad eaves on the lee-ward side of the house. Now the comforting crackle and hum of the burning wood provided a cheerful contrast to the eerie wail of the wind.

Nina didn't consider herself superstitious, but something about this storm was making her more than usually apprehensive. She didn't think it was just that she had always hated thunderstorms, nor was it fear of being alone in the cottage. She preferred it that way. In choosing to settle in such an out-of-the-way place, not easily accessible to the rest of the world, she had eagerly accepted a largely solitary way of life that enabled her to devote herself entirely to her painting.

Nine months ago, she had arrived on the island rootless, drifting, searching... In Puriri Bay she had found what she believed she had been looking for: a quiet refuge where she could rediscover her passion to paint. Here she could work long hours with no interruptions, no petty distractions...

Well, *almost* none, she thought as she stooped to switch on a lamp and spotted the damp black nose cautiously part-ing the fringed hem of the ivory throw rug that draped the elderly couch.

'You feel it, too, huh?' she murmured, snapping her fin-gers invitingly. The only response was a swift withdrawal of the quivering nose back under the sagging couch. 'It's probably just the build-up of static electricity in the air,' Nina reassured them both loudly, dismissing her vague pre-monition as the product of her overactive imagination.

As she straightened, she caught sight of her reflection in the glass door and pulled a wry face. She had pinned her hair up out of the way while she worked, but now she saw that the humidity had frizzed her wavy, dark chestnut locks into a mass of corkscrew curls that had sprung from her careless topknot.

Hands on hips, she studied her slightly pear-shaped outline in the darkened glass. In the relaxed island environment, Nina had quickly lost the knack of worrying about her appearance. Dressing for comfort rather than style saved her both time and money. Fortunately, the casual, fresh-scrubbed look seemed to suit her although she didn't consider herself more than ordinarily pretty.

At twenty-six she was resigned to the fact that her five-foot-six-inch frame had a genetic predisposition to carrying a little extra weight around her hips and thighs. But at least she had the consolation of knowing that the layer of padding was muscle rather than flab, she thought, twisting sideways and slapping a taut, denim-covered buttock, smugly confirming the lack of wobble. She did a lot of walking and cycling around the hilly island, and the fact that there was no fast-food joint within twelve nautical miles was a major encouragement to maintaining a healthy diet!

Thinking about food made her suddenly realise that she was peckish, and she wondered what she could come up with for dinner. Nina usually cooked for Ray, as well, but since he was away visiting his married daughter for the weekend, she could eat on a whim. She didn't feel like making a meal from scratch, but maybe cooking would cure her attack of the jitters. There might be some leftovers she could throw together to create something interesting.

She crossed to the kitchen to see what was left in the fridge. Perhaps she would have a light snack now and a hot supper later. It wouldn't do to eat too early and then have the evening stretch endlessly ahead of her. At this rate she could be up all night. She might be able to read or listen to music if she turned the stereo up to full volume, but there was no point in going to bed while the storm was still blowing, not if she was going to just lie there in the dark, obsessing over every huff and puff that shook her house of sticks.

As soon as she opened the refrigerator door, there was a scrabble of claws on polished wood, and she glanced over her shoulder to see a speeding black-and-white bullet shoot out from beneath the couch and trace a curving trajectory around the bench that divided the kitchen from the rest of the room. Nina slammed the door again just in time to prevent the missile imbedding itself in the lower shelves of the fridge where she usually thawed frozen packs of meat and the occasional meaty bone.

'No!' she said sternly to the long-haired Jack Russell terrier, who was quivering with outrage at being deprived of his plunder. She pointed to the bowl on the floor by the back door that contained a few crumbs of rice-flecked dog biscuit and a forlorn fishbone. 'You've already had plenty to eat today. You'll get fat if you're fed on demand.'

The wiry little dog looked supremely unimpressed. He plunked his hindquarters down on the cold, patterned-vinyl floor in front of the fridge, his beady black eyes fixed hungrily on her face.

'It's no use looking at me like that,' she told him.

He raised one limp front paw and uttered a single, pitiful whine.

Nina rolled her eyes. 'Hollywood!' she scoffed.

He sank slowly down on his stomach, his muzzle settling on his crossed paws with what sounded suspiciously like a deep sigh. The jaunty white tail lay flaccid on the dark green floor as if too weak to wag.

Nina echoed his doggy sigh with one of her own. They both knew who was going to crack first. They had played this game many times before. Oh, well…she might as well throw him his tidbit now and stave off the reproachful looks and pathetic whines long enough for her to fill her own belly.

Before she could reopen the fridge, there was a particularly strong gust of wind and she heard the first flurry of raindrops tattoo against the corrugated-iron roof. The dog's drooping tail and ears pricked up, and the listless waif suddenly turned into an energised ball of barks, hurtling himself at the back door and scratching at the panels.

'Zorro!'

The little dog glanced back at Nina, the two oblong patches of black fur that surrounded his eyes looking uncannily like the mask of his dashing namesake as he ignored her compelling cry and continued to leap in front of the closed door, barking madly.

Nina almost preferred him cowering under the couch.

'For goodness' sake, Zorro, calm down. It's only the rain.' She pulled aside the kitchen curtain to peer outside as she spoke, then saw what the dog must have sensed—a shadowy figure coalescing out of the darkness.

Someone was stumbling down the narrow, dead-end road that provided the only vehicle access to the bay. It was a steep, zigzagging road that turned sharply at the bottom of the hill just behind Nina's cottage and then ran along the flat to the public parking area at the far end of the beach.

Nina cupped her hand to the side of her face and squinted through the rain-smeared glass, her breath fogging the cold surface. Wrapped in a long, flapping coat and bent over against the wind, one hand lifted to protect against the rain that was driving in under the overhanging trees, the tall, bulky figure could have been either a man or a woman.

It obviously wasn't one of Nina's neighbours. A local would have been walking along the middle of the road, regardless of the risk of traffic, rather than on the unstable margin. Even in dry weather the ungraded road was inclined to be slippery along the edges where loose gravel collected in drifts. Nina only hoped that the visitor didn't end up sliding into the open ditch that ran alongside the road.

'Forget it, Zorro. No-one's going to come visiting us in this kind of weather,' she said to the cacophony of barks. 'It's just someone on their way to the Petersons or the Freemans—or maybe they just want to check on a boat.'

The barking stopped abruptly, and she was pleasantly surprised at this unprecedented act of instant obedience until she looked around and saw the flapping cat door. The round hinged panel had been installed by some past resident who owned an obviously hefty feline, and Zorro had been quick to appreciate its advantages.

'Dammit, Zorro!' Out the window she could see the little dog scampering past the letterbox and up onto the road, staggering sideways with each pummelling gust of wind. 'Oh, for heaven's sake!' Nina yanked open the door to call the dog back, and as she did so, two things happened simultaneously.

A sizzling bolt of blinding white light exploded out of the sky, striking the tallest roadside tree in a shower of sparks; and the rain flurries suddenly turned into a torrential deluge.

Momentarily dazzled by the lightning and disorientated by the ear-shattering thunder that followed barely a split second later, Nina didn't at first register the danger. But then, through the dark blur of the sheeting rain, she saw the smoking top of the puriri tree begin to peel away from the main trunk, leaving a pale, jagged stump pointing accusingly at the sky. As it toppled, gravity took over and the heavy thicket sheered completely off, plummeting through the threshing branches towards the puny human on the road below.

Her scream of warning was ripped away from her lips, lost to the wind and rain and the echoing roll of thunder as another lethal lightning bolt ripped into the ground farther up the hill. The flash of incandescence momentarily illuminated the ghastly scene, and Nina was forced to watch helplessly as the treetop crashed to the ground, obliterating its victim from view. At the last moment, the rain-lashed figure became aware of what was about to happen but dodged too late to escape the crushing impact.

Nina's feet unfroze and she dashed out into the maelstrom. She had barely gone a few steps before she was soaked to the skin, the rain drumming savagely down on her exposed head, the punishing drops beating into her eyes and mouth so that she could scarcely see or breathe as she splashed through the rivers of water, gravel and mud streaming down the road.

She could see Zorro, still barking fiercely, his scrawny flanks wet and heaving as he dashed up and down, making little darting forays at the fallen tree, clearly trying to get at the motionless bundle of clothes barely visible beneath.

Nina yelled at him to keep out from under her feet as she panted to a halt and began hauling on the tangled treetop, fighting against the wind and the sheer weight of the densely matted branches.

'Hey—can you hear me? Are you all right?' she shouted, tearing frantically at the barrier. 'I'm going to get you free. Can you move?' There was no reply, but she didn't give up, screaming a barrage of questions as she worked, hoping that the sound of her voice would jolt the trapped figure into a fighting awareness of what she was trying to do.

The coarse central trunk was thicker than her thigh and she found it difficult to get a grip. The wet bark kept slipping through her clumsy fingers as she tried to wrestle it aside, spiky stumps rasping and cutting at her hands, leaving dark trails of blood against her white palms. Bent twigs jabbed and scratched at her exposed skin and clusters of leathery leaves slapped against her face as she squatted low and edged in under the dripping mass, wedging a shoulder into a V-shaped fork in the trunk in the hope of being able to lever up the lighter end and roll it away.

Through the foliage that was whipping dangerously close to her eyes, Nina was able to catch an occasional glimpse of a pale, oval blur, reassuring her that at least the victim wasn't pinned facedown in the mud and in imminent danger of suffocation or drowning.

Spitting out mouthfuls of rainwater, Nina gritted her teeth and bent to her task with renewed urgency. Zorro skittered between her braced legs, squirming under the thicket of branches as soon as they began to lift off the ground, emerging backwards with the hem of a thick black coat gripped between his teeth. As he stretched the trapped fabric taut, Nina heard a harsh, masculine groan emerge from the depths of the tree. A burst of adrenalin gave her a moment of superhuman strength and she arched upright in a heaving twist, rolling the heavy trunk clear of the man sprawled on the gravel.

Nina fell to her knees beside him, catching his hand as it rose to waver in the air in front of his face as if groping for something that only he could see.

A sharp tingle shot up her arm and into her chest when their wet fingers touched, and she wondered whether his body had been harbouring some residual electricity from the lightning strike. She fought the desire to recoil, her hand tightening around his as she looked down into his square-jawed face, his features barely distinguishable in the rain-blurred darkness. There was nothing familiar about him. Nothing at all. The contraction in Nina's chest increased, her breath squeezing painfully through her lungs as she was stricken by a nameless terror.

She tried to push it away. Whoever the man was, he was undoubtedly dazed and in pain, his eyes slitted against the rain, dark rivulets of either mud or blood, or a mixture of both, pouring down from his left temple to drip off his jaw into the upright collar of his thick coat.

Lightning bolted out of the sky again, providing Nina with a convenient justification for her mindless panic, and she threw herself across the man's torso in an instinctive attempt to shield him from fresh harm.

His sharp groan of agony wrenched her back on her heels, her hands quickly searching over the front of his coat, the thickness of the dense weave frustrating her attempts to find the source of his pain. It was impossible to tell what his build was beneath the bulky coat, but he was certainly over six feet tall, and Nina knew that if he couldn't get down the hill under his own steam, she was going to have to go for help.

She put her mouth close to his ear, the fat, wet tails of her hair briefly pasting themselves against his lean cheek. 'Can you tell me where you're hurt?'

His head whipped around towards her voice, his hard temple colliding painfully with her high cheekbone.

'Ouch!' She cupped her eye, involuntary tears mingling with the raindrops on her lashes. As if she wasn't wet enough!

'What happened?' They were the first words he had uttered, and to her relief, his deep, harsh voice sounded thankfully lucid.

This time, Nina pulled back to where he would be able to see, as well as hear, the words on her lips. 'You were hit by a tree. We really need to get out of this storm and take a look at your injuries,' she told him. 'Are you able to move? My house is just down the hill.'

Instead of answering her, he rolled over onto his side and began to struggle awkwardly to his feet, hampered by the long, wet coat flapping around his legs. Nina hovered nervously, hoping that his movements weren't exacerbating a chest or back injury. He would be extremely lucky if he escaped with only minor cuts and bruises. As he straightened, he moaned and she slid her arm around the back of his waist, grateful that he appeared to be relatively steady on his feet. She prayed he would stay that way.

Man's best friend, satisfied that he had fulfilled his doggy duty, was already skittering back to his domain, his jaunty flag of a tail proclaiming that he confidently expected to dine a hero. Nina urged her companion in the same direction by pointing out the rectangle of light projected by the back door, which she had left open.

'Do you think you can make it that far?' It had really been a rhetorical question and she was startled to hear a low, sardonic rumble float over her head.

'Do I have a choice?'

If he could manage sarcasm under these conditions, then he couldn't be *that* badly injured, she reasoned.

'Well, yes, you could just stand here and wait for lightning to strike twice!'

Ten minutes later, Nina was perched on the edge of her couch, icy bare toes curling into the sheepskin hearthrug under her feet, her wet clothes steaming in the heat from the fire as she gently mopped at the blood that streaked one side of the injured man's face. The continual washing of rain had obviously kept the blood from clotting, and she was worried that it was still seeping in a steady flow from the gash just above his dark hairline.

Fortunately, he had managed to remove his muddy shoes and shed his heavy black coat in a sodden puddle on the floor before he had gracefully keeled over onto the oversoft couch. The rest of his clothes appeared only mildly damp, except for the muddy lower half of his black trousers.

He had lain sprawled on his back, his eyes closed, his breath coming in a harsh rattle between tightly drawn lips, as Nina had raced for a bowl of hot water, disinfectant and towels—one of which she had tucked under his wet head.

He hadn't moved when she had gingerly checked him over for other obvious wounds and started to clean his face, and at the moment she wasn't quite sure whether he was unconscious or merely limp with pain and exhaustion—but either way it gave her a chance to study him unobserved and soothe the nerves that had been jangling discordantly since she had first looked into his face up there on the hill.

There was nothing familiar about him to disturb her now. Nothing to make her heart quicken with uncomfortable anxiety. He was simply a stranger. A dangerously good-looking stranger, it was true—perhaps that was where the feeling of threat had sprung from.

Nina estimated him to be in his mid-thirties and even in repose his face had a kind of lean and hungry look to it. His fine-grained skin, which had merely been a pale glimmer out in the darkness, was actually a burnished gold beneath the surface chill, the olive undertones allied to the jet-black lashes and flared brows.

His hair fell back from a slight widow's peak above the faintly lined forehead, the wet strands melting into the white towel under his head drying to a natural blue-black sheen that made her guess that his eyes would be similarly dark.

His classic bone structure was the kind that would age well, she thought, the blade-straight nose perfectly proportionate to the wide-set eye sockets, high forehead and sculpted jaw. His smooth-shaven cheeks were faintly concave, his upper lip a thin, barely shaped line while the lower was pulled into noticeable fullness by the slashing indentation in his chin, far too masculine to be called a dimple.

His dark colouring was accentuated by the fact that he was dressed all in black—a knitted rollneck sweater tucked into the flat waistband of his pleated trousers, both close-fitting enough to reveal a body that was long and rangy, the lean, triangular torso tapering to narrow hips and long-boned thighs.

Here in the light, his colour of choice threw him into sharp relief against the ivory throw rug. Her artist's imagination visualised him as a thin streak of black over a ripple of changing textures.

Shadow man...

To Nina, black was a symbol of complexity—a subtle, sensuous, secretive colour. She never bought it in a tube, preferring to mix it up herself on her palette, so she knew that there were many shades of black, rich with the potential to refract just a tiny portion of incidental light and thereby alter the viewers' perception of what they were seeing from moment to moment. Black was an optical trick, an illusion.

But the man on her couch was no illusion. Nina shivered as she leaned forward to dab at a fresh welling of blood, her trembling fingers almost dropping the crimson-stained towel.

He winced, his head rolling to the side, knocking her hand away, his eyes flicking open. It gave her an odd shock to see they weren't the dark brown suggested by his swarthy colouring, but an extremely light blue, like floes of ice packing in around his shrinking pupils, and her heart accelerated unevenly in her chest.

'Oh, it's you,' he said thickly, his voice as surly as his frown.

'Who did you expect it to be?' Nina resumed her dabbing. 'Your guardian angel?'

'I don't believe in angels.'

Somehow she wasn't surprised by the flat pronouncement. The faint tracery of laughter lines at the outer corners of his eyes suggested that he was capable of good-natured whimsy, but the cynical brackets that had appeared around his compressed mouth revealed a more dominating trait.

'Then you shouldn't tempt fate when God is flinging thunderbolts about,' she told him. 'You could have been badly injured.'

'Tempting fate is what I do best,' he murmured.

She wasn't impressed. 'Well, miracle man, you certainly came off second-best this time, didn't you?' she pointed out, removing the towel and carefully parting the matted hair at his temple.

He moaned at the slight pull on the edges of the open wound. 'What are you doing?' His head winced away from her on the cushion and he put a hand up to his forehead.

'That falling tree gashed your scalp,' she explained, wondering how much of the accident he actually remembered. 'I'm cleaning it up so I can see how deep the cut is.'

He lowered his hand and stared at his stained fingertips. 'I'm bleeding like a stuck pig,' he groaned.

'Scalp wounds are like that,' she said bracingly. Men were such babies when it came to their physical hurts. 'From what I can see, the cut's shallow but it's quite long. You may need a few stitches to hold it together.'

His eyes had fluttered closed. 'Bitch!' he muttered.

'I was only offering an opinion.' Nina tried not to take the insult personally. If his mind was suffering the lingering effects of a blow to his head, she couldn't expect him to obey the usual rules of polite conversation. Perhaps his comment had been aimed at some other female who had suddenly flitted into his hazed brain. 'I wasn't threatening to darn you up myself. How are you feeling...apart from the head, I mean?'

'You were copping a free feel a few minutes ago. You tell me,' he said without opening his eyes.

She flushed at his raw imagery. So he had been fully cognisant all along...thank goodness she hadn't lingered over her task! In the circumstances, it had been the practical thing to do, but it had still seemed uncomfortably intimate.

Moulding the stranger's muscles through his chilled clothes, she had found it impossible to remain as detached as she would have liked.

'I was just checking to see whether you had any obvious broken bones,' she defended herself. Since his eyes had been closed then, too, he couldn't have possibly known her eyes had strayed where her touch had dared not....

'I'm never obvious. Discretion is my middle name.' He made it sound like a sinful accomplishment.

'What's your first?'

'Hmm?' His thick lashes rose to half-mast, showing a sliver of blue bemusement. 'My first what? First woman?'

Nina felt a surprising kick of fury. She flicked back her heavy mane of wet hair in a gesture of haughty disdain. She didn't know why he thought she might be interested in his sexual peccadilloes.

'No—your first *name*. Who are you? My name is Nina— Nina Dowling,' she repeated emphatically, anxious to extract a response before he lost the thread of the conversation again. 'What's *yours?* What are you doing in Puriri Bay? Is there someone who's going to be worried if you don't turn up?'

'Nina?' He seemed confused by her string of questions, unable to concentrate sufficiently to answer any of them. She placed a flat hand against his hard cheek and moved her face closer to his, silently demanding he give her his full attention. He blinked up into her worried green eyes, his pupils visibly expanding, melting the circles of blue ice to a silvery rim of frost. 'Nina...' His gaze sank to the tiny mole just above the neat pink bow of her mouth. 'It's you,' he said in a tone of deep satisfaction.

Except for his lack of surliness, they were right back where they had started, Nina realised in exasperation. He was looking at her as if he expected congratulations for his

simple act of recognition. 'Yes, that's right, it's me, Nina—
I just told you that. But who—are—*you?*'

She separated each word to stress the vital importance
of the question.

'Who am I?' he repeated equally slowly, a disturbing
blankness beginning to steal across his face, wiping it clean
of all expression.

Her fingers tensed against his hard cheek, keenly aware
of the strength—and the terrifying fragility—of the skull
beneath the skin.

'Don't you *know?*' she asked, trying not to let her panic
leak into her voice.

His silence was echoed in his empty eyes, and her hand
flew up to cover her appalled mouth.

'Oh, God, you have no idea, do you?' she said in a shattered whisper. 'You can't tell me who you are because you
don't even remember your own name!'

CHAPTER TWO

THE stranger's eyelids drooped and Nina's stomach hollowed with fear. Wasn't excessive drowsiness supposed to be a bad sign? What if he lapsed into a coma?

'Hey!' She shook him by the shoulder, trying not to jar his head. 'Open your eyes—you can't go to sleep now!'

'Why not? You planning on turfing me back out into the storm?' he roused himself to challenge, still wearing the alarmingly vacant expression that persuaded her it would do little good to keep pressing him about his identity. At this point, it might even be dangerous to get him overagitated about his condition.

'Of course not, but you could have a bit of concussion,' she told him. She had been far too ready to assume that because he was walking and talking after the accident his injuries were superficial. But what if she was wrong? She, of all people, should know how unpredictable a seemingly minor bump on the head could be....

Unfortunately, as far as getting help was concerned, her options were severely limited. Emergency services were out; there were none on the island—not even a practising GP—and for the duration of the storm they were effectively cut off from the mainland. Even the rescue helicopter would be grounded. Ray had left her his key so she could dash over there and use his telephone, but she didn't like the idea of having to leave the injured stranger alone in unfamiliar surroundings. Besides, whom would she call?

Who amongst her other close neighbours was likely to be useful? It was no use running off to beg help from someone who was just as ignorant as herself. But at this time of year the candidates were pathetically few.

Almost all of the houses in Puriri Bay were weekenders, and when the weather forecast had been so wretched, most of the owners would have flagged away their weekly pilgrimage to the island. During the winter, the neighbourhood was frequently reduced to a few hardy old-timers and some casual renters with whom Nina had only a nodding acquaintance.

But the Freemans were here! Her back straightened as she recalled seeing their distinctive, shiny green four-wheel drive roll off the ferry the previous day when she had walked over to the jetty to wave Ray off and pick up a mail-order package from the post-box at the store.

Although Nina didn't know Dave Freeman particularly well herself—he was only an intermittent visitor to his bach—he was a long-time fishing buddy of Ray's and she knew that he freely gave the older man advice on his arthritis. He was actually a psychiatrist, but shrinks were medical doctors in the first instance, weren't they? Just because she had been stand-offish to him in the past was no reason to be reluctant to approach him now. While Shearwater Islanders were fiercely respectful of each other's right to privacy—that was why the island was such a haven for social misfits—in a crisis their community spirit was invariably staunch.

She jumped up and found herself tethered to the couch by a hand that had shot out with surprising speed to fist in the saturated denim bagging around her knee.

'Where are you going?'

'Nowhere,' she soothed, easing the bunched fabric out of his grasp, taken aback by the raw suspicion in his voice. 'But I've just thought of someone who can give me some advice about that gash on your head.' She raised her voice. 'Zorro, come here!'

The little dog came trotting out of the kitchen, dragging the discarded soup bone that Nina had used to distract him from chewing on the stranger's muddy shoes.

A faint, choking sound floated up from the couch. 'You're going to ask a *dog* for a medical opinion!'

His incredulous outrage sent a buzz of amusement humming through her veins, easing the pressure of her intense anxiety.

'Unfortunately, he's not licensed to practise.' Nina removed the bone from the dog's mouth and picked up the gnawed handle of an expensive fishing rod from the bookcase, holding it out for Zorro to sniff.

'You know where you got this, don't you, boy?' she said encouragingly. 'Dr Freeman—*Dave*—gave it to you after you kept stealing it off his back porch at Christmas. You take it along with you when Dave takes you and Ray out fishing on his boat, and he throws this in the water for you, doesn't he?'

Nina was scribbling a brief line on a scrap of paper and taping it to the stumpy rod as she spoke. 'You like playing fetch with Dave, don't you?' She mimed a throwing action and the terrier began to prance energetically. Nina crouched down and looked into the beady masked eyes as she placed the piece of rod firmly between his jaws. 'I want you take this along to Dave's place now. I want you to *fetch—Dave!* Understand?'

Zorro pricked up his ears, his whine mingling with a sleepy snort from the patient.

'Of course he can't understand—he's a dog!'

Nina bristled in defence of her companion. 'Zorro is extremely intelligent. He knows what I'm saying, don't you, boy? You're going to play *fetch* with *Dave*.'

The Jack Russell barked excitedly around the edges of the rod and took off at his customary velocity.

As his claws clicked across the kitchen floor, Nina re-

membered to call out, 'Uh, Zorro, just don't forget that the
rod may not—' There came a sharp rap and a pained whine,
followed by a furious rattling and growling. '—fit cross-
ways through the cat door.' The fight sounds rose to a cres-
cendo of frustrated snarls and Nina was about to dive to
the rescue when there was a scraping *pop* and a series of
muffled, triumphant yips diminishing into the distance.

'Extremely intelligent, huh?'

Nina ran her hands through her wringing-wet hair, scoop-
ing it off her clammy neck. 'He tends to leap before he
looks sometimes, but even intelligent *humans* do that,' she
pointed out.

'You really expect him to do it?' he wondered.

Rather than following the upward movement of her arms,
the blue eyes had drifted in the opposite direction. Nina
looked down to see her drenched sweatshirt plastered to her
uplifted breasts, shaping their modest fullness and explicitly
revealing her lack of a bra. She hastily plucked the wrinkled
fabric away from her unpleasantly chilled skin. 'I know he
will. Zorro's very dedicated when he thinks he's on a mis-
sion,' she said more confidently than she actually felt. She
wouldn't relish going back out into the storm herself. 'In
the meantime, I'm going to get into some dry clothes.'

'Don't bother on my account.'

His mocking drawl made her cold nipples tingle with
embarrassment. She had taken her body for granted for so
long that it was a shock to find it responsive to a casual
male comment, particularly in such inappropriate circumstances.

'Just keep that towel pressed against your head until I
get back!'

She would have liked to have a shower, but the thought
of standing naked under a steamy flow of water with the
silver-eyed stranger just the other side of the wall made her
insides turn over. Instead, she managed to change top and

bottom without ever being completely nude, towelling herself roughly and pulling on dry underwear, including a sturdy white cotton bra, woollen stretch pants and a roomy checked shirt with the sleeves rolled up. She blotted her hair and rubbed it with a towel before fastening it high on her head in a loose ponytail that would enable it to dry naturally without getting totally out of control.

She needn't have worried about her unexpected guest wandering in on her shower. When she returned to the lounge after dumping her wet clothes in the laundry tub, he was still lying on the couch in exactly the same position, eyes closed, towel obediently clamped to his temple.

She felt a brief tremor of uncertainty at his stillness but relaxed when she picked up the steady rise and fall of his chest. The battering gusts of wind and roaring barrage of rain on the iron roof masked her movements as she quietly picked up his bunched coat from the floor, surprised at its weight, the musty smell of wet wool clogging her nostrils as she carried it into the bathroom and draped it over the curtain rail of the shower.

Turning to leave, she hesitated, then, feeling guilty, explored each of the pockets in turn. She found no wallet, but in one of the deep side pockets she found a bunch of keys, and from the breast pocket in the grey silk lining she drew out an elegant silver cigarette lighter, sculpted in voluptuous lines that stressed art over pure functionality.

It was agreeably heavy, fitting perfectly in the hollow of her hand, the smooth metal cool to the touch as it rested on her open palm. Her fingers closed possessively around the curving shape and she battled an unexpectedly compelling urge to slip it into her own pocket.

Appalled by her unaccustomed craving, Nina hurried out to rid herself of the temptation, dropping the keys quietly onto the table by the couch and placing the cigarette lighter carefully beside it.

She glanced over at the recumbent figure as she did so and her heart jerked in her chest as she found him quietly watching her, his narrowed blue eyes moving between the articles on the table and the naked oval of her face.

She moistened her dry lips. 'Uh, I emptied the pockets of your coat so I could hang it up to dry,' she explained, inwardly squirming at the lie. 'I found these....'

As her fingers reluctantly withdrew from the seductive contours of the lighter, her thumb smoothed over a slight roughness in the casing. It could have been the jeweller's mark, but Nina knew with a hitch in her breathing that it wasn't a silver stamp the sensitive pad of her thumb was identifying. Sure enough, when she tilted it to the light, she found herself looking down at a brief inscription in flowing letters, too small to read at arm's length.

'What's the matter?' In spite of his air of exhausted confusion, he was alert enough to notice her subtle change of expression.

'There's an engraving...' she began, torn between her intense curiosity and the need to deny the powerful allure of the silver talisman.

'Is there?' No spark of enlightenment ignited his gaze. 'Well—what does it say?' he prompted, struggling up on one elbow as the seconds ticked by and she made no attempt to read the tiny inscription.

She bit her lip as she held it up, her dark lashes fanning down like sable brushes over her troubled green eyes, painting out his view of their expression.

'"*For Ryan, the bright foreigner in my life,*"' she read, and frowned as she tried to make sense of the cryptic words, grappling with an elusive sense of familiarity. The inscription was put there by a woman, she was sure, but its meaning continued to lie stubbornly just beyond her comprehension.

'What does it mean? Foreigner in what way? Do you think it means that you're not a New Zealander?'

She was aware of him slumping back against the cushion. 'I have no idea,' he murmured, his voice so flat with disappointment that she knew he spoke the absolute truth.

But at least she now had one clue as to his identity. 'Ryan...' She tested it out on her tongue, hoping the sound of it might trigger his memory. 'Ryan must be your first name—does it ring any bells?'

'I...my head...'

'Is it hurting more?'

She broke off, relieved by the thumping on the back door, which heralded the arrival of an oilskin-clad Dave Freeman with a rather subdued-looking dog tucked under one arm and a briefcase under the other.

'Oh, God, Dr Freeman—what happened!' she gasped.

'I thought that was my line,' he said, smiling wryly, handing Zorro over as the wind whisked the door out of Nina's hand and slammed it shut with a violent bang behind them. 'He's okay. He just got bowled over by the wind when he jumped out of the Range Rover. It's only his pride that's hurt,' he explained.

'Good boy, Zorro!' Nina praised him extravagantly as she put him down on his wobbly legs and patted his wet head. She was so grateful that he had fulfilled his urgent commission that she didn't even chide him when he shook himself violently, splattering muddy water over her stretch pants. 'I was a bit worried that with the racket going on outside you might not hear him barking,' she admitted.

'We didn't at first, not until he jumped up onto the front deck and attacked the French doors. Persistent little beggar, isn't he? I know he's not too keen on storms, so I figured that it wasn't his idea to play fetch in the middle of a gale!'

'I'm sorry to drag you out on such a filthy night,' Nina said anxiously as her visitor briskly shouldered out of his hooded coat and hung it on the back of the door, 'but I couldn't think of what else to do.'

She hastily explained what had happened while Dave Freeman washed his hands at the kitchen sink. He was not much taller than her, but broad and stocky, still physically vigorous in his mid-fifties. With his balding grey head, chubby round face and neat silver beard, he had the look of a kindly teddy bear, but Nina had always found his rock-steady brown gaze uncomfortably penetrating.

Now, she was grateful for their unwavering calmness as she recounted her tale.

'His clothes are a bit damp, but I didn't like to move him around too much while his head was bleeding. He seems to have no idea who he is and that made me worry that he might have some kind of skull fracture or something.'

He dried his hands on the clean towel she handed him from the airing cupboard.

'Well, there's not an awful lot we could do about that right now except keep him under observation until the weather clears enough to get him to a hospital,' he said gravely. 'But let's not get ahead of ourselves. The worst-case scenario is often the least likely.'

He opened his briefcase and took out a stethoscope, his gravity lightening when he saw Nina's expression of ill-disguised relief.

'It's not exactly the traditional black bag, but I always carry a very well-equipped first-aid kit around with me.' He looped the stethoscope around his neck and patted it against his chest. 'My badge of office—reassurance to the patient I'm not just any port in a storm—even though in this case it's literally true. Do you think I look enough like a real doctor?'

'But I thought... That is, you *are* one, aren't you?' Nina said, disconcerted by his flippancy.

'Quite. So you can safely leave your injured stranger in my hands. I promise I'll give him a thorough going-over.'

'Oh, yes, of course.' She was flustered as she realised he was gently suggesting that he preferred to conduct his examination alone. 'He's through here on the couch, Doctor—although you can use one of the spare bedrooms if you want to be more private.'

'You may as well call me Dave,' he said, grinning. 'No point in us being formal when Zorro and I are already on first-name terms.'

Leaving the two men together, Nina hastily made herself scarce, bundling Zorro along to the bathroom where she cleaned his paws and gave his ecstatic body a hot bath of air with her hair dryer, running her fingers through the soft fur until it was silky dry again, shedding a lot of sand and grit on the floor in the process.

Thanks to the sound of the hair dryer allied with the wind and the rain, Nina was protected from the ignominy of eavesdropping on the proceedings in the living room, but she was quick to appear the instant that Dave called her name.

She was unaware that she was clenching her hands at her sides until he greeted her with his affable smile, spreading his big hands in their white latex gloves. 'Well, he seems to have escaped with just a few bumps and bruises, but you were right about his cut needing a couple of stitches. Would you mind acting as my nurse for a few minutes?'

Her white knuckles relaxed and she flexed her fingers, the fierce tingling a signal that the blood was returning to her cramped muscles.

'No, of course not.' She transferred her gaze to the patient and found his eyes on her betraying hands. His face looked a little greyer than it had been when she left the room, and a lot more shuttered. 'That is, if *you* don't mind...'

His head lifted and a ghost of a smile drifted across his pale lips. 'Why should I? You've played nurse pretty convincingly so far. I doubt you're going to see anything you haven't seen already.'

That wasn't quite true. Although he now had the thick mohair snuggle rug that had been folded on the arm of her chair tucked over his long body, his shoulders were bare above it, and the trousers lying on top of his sweater on the floor told Nina that the examination had been every bit as thorough as promised.

She couldn't help noticing that the black hair that swirled on his deep chest looked as soft and luxuriant as the strokeable mohair or that his lean shoulders and upper arms, lying exposed on top of the blanket, were smoothly contoured with well-defined muscle even when relaxed.

Her gaze sweeping down the bronzed forearms covered with superfine black hair to the slender hands clasped loosely on his flat abdomen, she saw for the first time that he was wearing a black digital watch and a discreet gold signet ring, inset with jade, on the little finger of his right hand.

Tearing her eyes away from the unexpected impact of his masculinity, Nina busied herself getting the supplies Dave requested as he ripped open a sterile pack from his bag. She felt a little tug of protest when he borrowed her razor to shave a thin strip from the edge of his patient's dark hairline, but he chuckled that it would soon grow back.

'No sign of male-pattern baldness yet, you lucky dog,' he said. 'I was thinning before I hit thirty-five. I would guess you're somewhere around that yourself.'

He didn't wait for an answer but swabbed the patch with a topical anaesthetic, apologising for the lack of anything stronger to block the pain.

'We don't want to take a chance of numbing any of your other responses for the next few hours.'

Nina winced unconsciously as he poised the needle and surgical thread at the edge of the wound, the bowl of cottonwool balls and pair of sterilised scissors she was holding, sagging in her grasp.

Dave paused, raising grey eyebrows at her. 'Okay?'

She braced her shoulders. '*I* am,' she said, glancing down at the stranger's set face, his eyes fixed blankly on some distant point in the room.

'Ryan will be, too. He's in pretty good physical shape for someone who's just been beaten up by a tree, so I'd say he's tough enough to weather a few little pinpricks.'

'You're calling him Ryan—did he remember that was his name?' she blurted, leaning forward eagerly.

'He's still hazy on personal details, but he told me about the lighter,' he replied, disappointing her, his brown eyes delivering a silent caution. 'So we've decided Ryan is more likely than John Doe and less melodramatic than Mr X.'

Nina bit her lip and forced herself to stand back. The man suffering the suturing didn't even twitch a muscle. He seemed to have retreated somewhere deep inside himself where pain could not reach. But that would require a mental control that he didn't seem to possess right now, so perhaps his state of confusion had deepened to the point that the pain receptors in his brain simply weren't accepting any more messages from his abused body.

'Very neat,' she said shakily as she watched Dave cut the final thread and carefully sealed the bloody needle and soiled swabs into a thick waste packet.

The unflattering surprise must have shown in her voice for he cut her his wry grin.

'Actually, I do needlepoint as a hobby—not very macho, but it helps me relax. The only trouble is that I'm so good at it my wife makes me do all our darning!'

Since Ray had told her that the Freemans were loaded, Nina took his last comment with a pinch of salt.

'How are you feeling now, Ryan?' Dave shone his pen light into the blue eyes.

'Like some sadist just used me for needlepoint practice!' came the grim reply.

Dave laughed. 'Well, you can relax now and have a good rest—the sadist is leaving. Nina here will look after you. We'll see how you are in the morning. My bet is that by then you'll be a different man.'

Ryan's grim expression flattened into serene calm. 'I have no doubt you're right.'

Nina was not so sanguine and she followed Dave back into the kitchen with her doubts. 'So you definitely don't think he's got a fracture?' she said in a low voice.

'Without an X-ray I can't totally rule it out,' he began cautiously, 'but, no, I'm pretty sure he doesn't. Although he's displaying a disordered state of consciousness that suggests concussion, there's nothing to indicate any serious underlying brain injury. He's dizzy but not nauseous, and while his verbal responses are mixed, his motor responses are all good. The deep bruising on his forearms looks like a defence injury, so I suspect he must have deflected a great part of the impact along his arms. The cut is just minor stuff and should heal with no trouble. I definitely couldn't find any suspicious bumps or depressions anywhere else on his skull.'

'But you do think he might have some minor concussion?' Nina pressed as he repacked his briefcase.

'I think you should keep an eye on him for the next twenty-four hours, just to be on the safe side. He can go to sleep if he wants to, but you should wake him every couple of hours. Turn on the light and make him open his eyes, see if he can talk lucidly and obey a few simple commands.'

'Don't you think you should stay?' she asked nervously.

'Look, I know you don't have a phone here—so take my

cell phone.' He handed it to her with succinct instructions on how to work it. 'And here's my number at the bach,' he said, scribbling it on the back of one of his business cards. 'If you have any problems or questions—whatever time it is—call me. Okay? And if any calls come through for me—just advise whoever it is to take two aspirin and call me in the morning!'

She didn't respond to his bracing good humour and he sobered.

'Tell me what's *really* bothering you.'

She turned the palm-sized phone over and over in her hands as she finally got to the crux of her concern. 'Surely you must be worried about the extent of his memory loss. He's going to completely freak out when the realisation hits him that his whole life is a void.'

Dave paused in doing up the latch of his briefcase, his eyes faintly compassionate. 'Is that what happened to you?'

She felt the tension build up along her spine, tightening all the connnective muscles along the way. This was why she had always avoided him in the past. She hadn't wanted to be the object of any professional curiosity. Word of mouth had inevitably made the bare bones of her story fairly common knowledge on the island, but in general people didn't poke their noses into your background unless you raised the subject with them yourself. There were too many Shearwater Islanders whose pasts wouldn't bear too close examination.

'It was totally different for me. I always knew exactly who I was. When I woke up from that bump on the head, I was still *me*. I didn't lose my entire identity…just a couple of unimportant years out of my life that I've shown I can perfectly well do without.'

She tossed her head carelessly, setting her damp ponytail swinging, but he didn't ask the question for which she was

unconsciously braced: how did she know they were unimportant if she couldn't remember them?

'And they're still lost?' His bushy eyebrows arched up.
'Since you've been living here you haven't experienced any
flashes of recall for the previous two years?'

The back of her neck itched. 'Nope. The only drawback
is that I sometimes have to remind myself that I'm two
years older than I feel,' she added flippantly, to show him
how little the whole thing bothered her.

Which was true. Nina didn't like to talk about the circumstances of her arrival on Shearwater Island, but that was
only because she was too busy with the exciting challenges
of the present to waste time looking back over her shoulder.
She certainly didn't need to consult a psychiatrist!

'Most women would envy your being able to honestly
deny remembering a couple of birthdays,' Dave agreed in
the same joking vein, reflecting her own attitude back at
her in a way that eased the fine tension from her body as
he continued. 'But you're right—Ryan's global amnesia *is*
different, although I'm sure it's only a temporary trauma.
He's a bit shocky, and that compounded with the concussion has probably scrambled the links between his memory
systems. It's a pretty classic pattern. After he has a good
rest and his system settles down, his ability to concentrate
should return, along with his memory.'

Nina felt she was learning more than she really wanted
to know about the mysteries of the brain. She had never
been one for clinical details, which was probably why she
tried to rule doctors and hospitals out of her life.

'Were you able to find out anything else about him?' she
asked, determined to keep the focus firmly back where it
belonged.

He plucked his beard thoughtfully. 'Well, he has a few
old scars—' he tilted his head roguishly '—but I think they
come under doctor-patient privilege. He couldn't say where

he'd come from or where he was going and we couldn't find any wallet in his clothing—maybe he lost it out there on the road. You're more familiar with who's living around here than I am at the moment. Are you certain you haven't seen him before, even casually?'

'I'm positive. He's a total stranger,' she said firmly. 'That was the first thing that struck me about him. Believe me, if I knew who this Ryan was, I'd leap at the chance to hand him over to whoever invited him to visit. I don't mind helping out in an emergency, but I'm really not prepared for a house guest right now.' She was aware that sounded selfish, but already the stranger had caused a disruption to her peaceful existence.

'Speaking of which—have you got something else he can wear, or should I bring some of my clothing over? He needs to keep warm to counteract the effects of shock.'

'I think I have a few things lying around that should fit him.' Karl had been the last person she had had to stay, and he was notoriously untidy with his possessions.

She half turned and her breathing shortened as she suddenly saw the man leaning against the corner where the living-room wall abutted the kitchen. How long had he been standing there listening? And how much of the conversation had he actually taken in? There was a guarded watchfulness in the blue eyes, a kind of baffled fury that made her think of a trapped animal.

And, without the mohair rug, there was nothing to disguise the animal-like sleekness of his body, streamlined with lithe and sinewy muscle, the thick tangle of hair on his chest tapering down to a narrow line where the broad band of elastic dipped low across his slim hips, the thin, stretchy, grey boxers softly clinging to contours of his masculinity.

Nina could feel her cheeks warm. She cleared her throat. 'I was just saying goodbye to the doctor.'

His intent stare didn't shift from her face. 'I need to use the bathroom,' he said bluntly.

'Oh...' Her blush deepened. 'It's straight down the hall, first on the right,' she said, pointing, and as he pushed himself away from the wall and shambled stiffly off in the right direction, she looked anxiously over her shoulder at Dave.

He grinned. 'His kidneys are working—that's definitely a very good sign.'

She decided that the psychiatrist was an incurable optimist by nature. 'Will he be all right by himself?' she worried.

He pursed his lips. 'Would you like me to check before I leave?'

'Yes, please. And then could you show him across the hall to the spare room? I'll make up the bed in there. It'll be much more comfortable than the couch.' If the storm was going to keep her awake, she didn't want to have to spend all night watching her uninvited guest sleep. Briefly looking in on him once every two hours would be much less taxing on the nerves!

CHAPTER THREE

A REVERBERATING crash wrenched Nina upright in her chair, her hand flattened against her pounding chest, a scream hovering in the back of her dry throat.

She blinked around the dimly lit room, half expecting to see that the roof had fallen in, but everything looked reassuringly normal. The fire had been reduced to glowing embers, and shifting her cramped legs under the mohair rug, she was surprised to realise that she must have nodded off despite the gale still rocking the house on its foundations.

At least the thunder and lightning at the leading edge of the storm had passed over. But the rain had barely eased, driving horizontally against the front of the house and drum-rolling across the roof to overflow the gutters in a noisy tattoo on the wooden decking below.

Perhaps the noise that had woken her had been a loose branch smashing against the creaking weatherboards. Zorro wasn't in his usual sprawl in front of the fire, and for a moment she was concerned until she remembered that he had surprisingly chosen to sacrifice his comfort to keep vigil over the stranger, curled up on the floor on the worn piece of sheepskin he used as a portable bed.

It was still pitch-black outside the rain-streaked window, and Nina turned her wrist, squinting down at her bare arm before she remembered that she wasn't wearing a watch. She hadn't made that slip in a very long time. She had broken her watch in her companionway fall on the ferry that had first brought her to Shearwater and in the months that followed had never taken the ferry company up on their offer to replace it. Only people who had to live to a schedule needed to carry around a constant reminder of their next appointment. Time was relative, and Nina preferred the more flexible version: island time. 'She'll be right, mate,' an islander would chuckle if someone missed the late-afternoon ferry sailing. 'There'll be another one along to-morrow!'

Nina looked over at the small driftwood clock on the stone mantelpiece above the sluggish fire. Barely 4:00 a.m.—still a little too soon to wake Ryan up again, she decided conscientiously. She picked up the book that had slipped off her lap and fallen face down on the floor. So far he had passed all the little tests that Dave had suggested with flying colours, and as the hours crept by, she had begun to rationalise her previous worries as absurdly excessive. Of course he would be all right. And in the clear light of day, they would establish exactly who he was and he would be happily, if not entirely healthily, on his way!

Suddenly, there was another crash and the unmistakable sound of shattering glass from along the hall, and she realised that the noise that had startled her out of her sleep had come from the same direction. The accompanying hoarse cry of her name galvanised her into action and she dashed down to the spare bedroom, her heart in her mouth.

Her hand scrabbled for the light-switch, and as the overhead light blazed into life, her gaze cut to the figure standing by the narrow single bed pushed against the far wall.

'Ryan, are you all right?' She didn't need to ask what had happened. The rudimentary lamp, made of a sand-filled chianti bottle topped off with a bare light bulb, was lying on the wooden floor, along with the upended pot plant that had sat next to it on the bedside cabinet, concealing the electric flex. Nearer to the edge of the bed lay the remains of a tall glass, the broken shards glinting wickedly in the widening pool of water seeping across the waxed floorboards. Zorro was warily skirting the debris, sniffing at the encroaching water.

'Nina?' Ryan lifted his hand to shade his eyes, narrowed against the sudden glare. 'It was dark…I couldn't find the lamp…I was thirsty.' His body swayed in her direction. 'Where were you?'

'Don't move!' Nina yelled as his bare foot left the ground and Ryan instantly froze in place, his eyes widening on her alarmed face, his pupils shrinking visibly to accommodate the light. 'Sorry,' she said, tempering her voice though still keeping it firm. 'But you might cut yourself. I don't want you to move until I clean up this broken glass.'

Well, he was certainly able to obey simple commands, she thought with grim amusement as he stood like a statue while she bustled around him with a dustpan and brush, pushing Zorro firmly away and sweeping up the glass and soil, mopping up the remains of the water with an old towel.

'I didn't know where you were,' he murmured as if it explained the mayhem, and perhaps it did. His mind had obviously fixed on Nina as the one constant in a dismayingly unfamiliar world. He must have woken in the dark and reached out for the reassurance of her presence, only to find that it wasn't there. She guessed from the husk of resentment in his voice that he didn't like being reliant on a stranger.

'I was only out in the living room,' Nina said as she put a fresh glass of water into his hand. 'Do you know where *you* are?'

'With you,' he said, giving her a look that was simultaneously sly and triumphant.

'No, I mean this *place?*'

He rubbed his head. 'That doctor with the needle—he told me about a bird—no, an island—a little island near

Auckland. But the bird was important, too....' He trailed off, and Nina supplied the detail that had eluded him.

'Shearwater Island.' At least he still vaguely remembered Dave amongst the jumble of half-finished thoughts.

'Shearwater Island,' he repeated in a dutiful monotone that gave her no confidence that it would stick in his mind.

He raised the glass to his dry lips and drank greedily, the strong column of his throat rippling, drawing Nina's fascinated gaze down to the hollow just above his collarbone where she could see the steady beat of his pulse.

Karl's faded, V-necked Auckland University sweatshirt was loose on Ryan's spare frame, sliding off one shoulder, and the soft, tan corduroy trousers were baggy in the legs and a few inches too short, but instead of making him look comical, the sloppy clothes seemed only to accentuate his air of natural arrogance. He was a man who was comfortable in his own skin, whatever he wore over it.

At first, however, he had baulked at putting on someone else's clothes.

'Whose are they?' he had demanded, glaring at them in suspicion when she had produced the shirt and pants from the chest of drawers in the corner of the room.

Granted, they were a bit shabby and no match for the designer labels on his own clothes, which had raised her eyebrows when she had inspected the washing instructions prior to throwing them into her machine, but there was no need for him to look as if he thought they might be crawling with vermin.

'They're perfectly clean,' she told him, shaking them out to prove it. 'And the man they belong to won't mind your borrowing them.'

'Who is he? Your *boyfriend?*' His emphasis made it sound like a sneer. 'You expect me to wear your lover's cast-offs?'

Nina tossed the clothes onto the bedspread and put her

hands on her hips, annoyed that he seemed to take it for granted that she didn't have a husband. Although, she supposed, he could have noticed her lack of a wedding ring....

'He's not my boyfriend. He's my foster-brother. And I'm only offering them to you because Dr Freeman said you needed to keep warm—'

'Your *brother?*' he interrupted in tones of harsh incredulity. His olive skin darkened, the flush of colour in his cheeks a startling contrast to their previous pallor.

The angry disbelief in his expression made Nina flush in turn. Now she was *really* getting annoyed. Did he think she was lying in order to hide the fact she had a lover? Was that why he flashed her that searing look of shocked fury? She never would have guessed him for a prude. No, it was more likely that he had mixed her up in his confused mind with somebody else.

She sighed. It would be best to keep her explanations simple and to the point.

'My *foster*-brother, Karl. He and I were brought up by my maternal grandparents. He works for a surfboard manufacturer in North Auckland now, but every so often he comes over to spend the weekend. And these are not cast-offs. He simply forgot to take them with him the last time he stayed. I happen to have bought that sweatshirt for him when he was at university—unfortunately, he majored in surfing rather than graduating with a degree!'

The feeble joke hadn't raised a smile, but Ryan's hostility had vanished as quickly as it appeared, and he had grudgingly accepted the proffered clothes.

Now, having drained the glass, he held it out to her, and as she took it, their fingertips brushed. 'My God, you're freezing!' she exclaimed in dismay, putting the glass down and cupping his chilled hands with hers. 'Look, why don't you get back into bed and I'll get you a hot-water bottle.'

She fetched him two, one for his cold feet and one to

clutch to his chest, but they didn't seem to be of any im-
mediate benefit. He lay hunched and shivering under the
covers as she piled on more blankets from the other spare
room until she was afraid he would be smothered under the
weight.

Zorro had padded back to his uneven square of sheepskin
and, after a ritual few turns, settled down with a snuffling
sigh of contentment. Nina envied him his easy slide into
canine oblivion. She had replaced the fused bulb in the
bedside light, but when she bent to switch it off, Ryan
jerked his head urgently off the pillow.

'No, leave the light on!'

'Oh, okay...' she acquiesced with an understanding
smile. She turned back towards the door and he stiffened
again.

'What are you doing—don't go!' He half rose on one
elbow, pushing back the heap of blankets.

'I won't be far away—'

'Nina, *no!*' He was getting out of bed again, and when
she hastily pushed him back, he captured her wrist in his
cold fingers. 'Stay here with me!'

His pale eyes burned with such a desperate intensity that
she quickly sought to ease his mind. 'All right, all right—
calm down. I'll stay...I promise.'

He seemed to find her solemn vow anything but reassuring. 'You promise?' he echoed with an ironic twist to
his mouth that hinted at a deeply cynical mistrust of human
nature.

She wished she knew what was going through his head.
'Yes.' She looked around the sparsely furnished room. 'Just
let me get something to sit on—'

'There's plenty of room here....' He used his free hand
to pull back the bedclothes as he scooted back in the bed,
tugging her forward until her knees hit the edge of the
mattress.

Nina stared wide-eyed at the inviting stretch of sheet, aware that she wasn't as shocked as she should be at the idea of sharing a bed with him. She had donned some socks, but she could still feel the chill striking up from the floorboards. Suddenly, she was hit by a wave of exhaustion. She had been up since seven the previous morning and the short nap in the chair only seemed to have increased the heavy lethargy dragging at her limbs. She half-heartedly tried to tuck the blankets back over his shivering body. 'Oh, I don't think so....'

Another coaxing tug on her wrist was accompanied by a persuasive whisper of pain. 'Please, I don't know what's happening to me, but I can't bear to be alone right now.'

The ache in his voice resonated in her empty heart, and without allowing herself to think any more about the wisdom of what she was doing, Nina sank onto the bed, sliding her strangely weighted legs down under the covers and resting her weary head on the cool pillow.

She lay on her side facing the room, as close to the edge of the bed as possible, but the dip in the soft mattress caused by the weight of the body behind her inevitably caused her to tip back towards the middle of the bed.

'Thank you...' he sighed, his warm breath tickling the back of her ear. His arm closed around her waist, drawing her back against his chest, the hot-water bottle trapped between them preserving the illusion of distance, its healing warmth melting the stiffness in Nina's lower back.

His knees butted into the back of her thighs, pushing them up into a relaxed curl, one bare foot tucking casually between her ankles. She could feel the rise and fall of his chest against her curved spine, the thud of his heart kicking into her shoulder-blade. Already his shivers were dying away as his face nuzzled into the thick waves tumbling down her back.

'Your hair is different,' he muttered.

He had only seen her looking like a frizzy drowned rat; Nina wished that was something that he *would* forget.

'I brushed it dry in front of the fire.' She had deliberately spun out the soothing task as a way of distracting herself from nature's destructive claws raking relentlessly at the house.

Now the raw fury of the storm didn't sound quite so frightening. Although she was the one supposedly offering comfort, she had discovered an unrecognised need in herself. How long had it been since she had lingered in the security of a warm human embrace? Karl was too self-absorbed to offer much in the way of comforting hugs and Nina had been so busy proving her independence that she had forgotten what it felt like to share the burden of a fear. She even found that she could now admit it out loud.

'I *hate* storms like this…especially when there's thunder and lightning, as well—they just terrify me.' She shuddered, the image of those death bolts slamming out of the boiling sky burned into her retina.

His arm tightened, his palm sliding farther under the curve of her ribs. 'I know, but you came out to help me anyway. That was brave.'

It had been fear, not bravery, that had driven her out into the storm—fear for him. 'How did you know I hate storms?'

There was no answer, and for a moment she wondered whether he had drifted back to sleep, but the quickening of his heartbeat suggested otherwise.

'Ryan?' she said sharply, the muscles pulling tight in her twisted neck as she squirmed her head around on the pillow in a vain attempt to see his face. Determined to find the answer, she loosened the arm at her waist and wriggled around to face him, wincing as their knees briefly collided. She straightened out her legs against the hard column of his thighs and flattened her hands on his chest to stop herself rolling farther into the hollow he had created in the mattress. Her hips were cushioned by the hot-water bottle that lay across his lower abdomen, branding the centre of their bodies with a fiery heat.

Their heads were level on the pillow, and as she had suspected, his deep-set eyes were open, a shimmer of blue under the heavy lids, his hair tousled dry by sleep, the short strands spraying out like fine black ink against the snowy whiteness of the pillowcase.

'How did you know that I'm afraid of storms?' she persisted cautiously, her green eyes searching for any sign of evasion.

His face was calm, his eyes steady. 'You were screaming your head off,' he said simply, resettling his arm over her waist, his hand splayed over the warm patch left on her lower back by contact with the hot-water bottle.

It was a perfectly reasonable assumption—however hesitant he was to frame it in words.

'That's because you weren't answering me.' She unconsciously spread her hand over his beating heart as she revisited those endless moments of nerve-grinding panic. 'At first I—I thought that you might be dead.'

'Would you have cared?'

The breath caught in her throat, her fingers clenching convulsively in the soft fabric of the sweatshirt. 'That someone had died? How can you ask that? Of course I would!'

'I meant me, specifically. If *I* died,' he murmured, increasing her agitation.

'I don't even know who *you*—specifically—are,' she denied quickly, anxious not to pursue his morbid train of thought. 'Do you realise you just remembered me screaming? Can you think back now? Do you remember what happened to you?'

'I remember what happened *afterwards*,' he corrected her. 'I remember opening my eyes and seeing you.'

'Oh.' Her disappointment was mingled with an uncomfortable surge of relief. Of course it would be less hassle if she could just treat him as a ship passing in the night, but even ships, she thought, have registered names...unless they were pirates out for plunder! He certainly had the colouring to be a buccaneer from the Spanish Main, but she couldn't detect any accent to his English.

She saw that his eyelids were slowly sinking again and couldn't resist the urge to test him.

'Ryan?' His lids flicked up and she smiled encouragingly at him. 'At least you seem to be responding to your name.'

'Yes, but I don't know whether that's because it really *is* my name or simply because you've *told* me it is,' he said wearily, and she immediately felt guilty.

'I'm sorry.' She bit her lip. 'I know I'm not supposed to pressure you—'

'No, *I'm* sorry...that I can't do what you want. I'm trying to remember, but when I do...my head feels as if it's about to explode.'

He couldn't have said anything more calculated to earn her compassion. She knew exactly how that felt. 'Then don't try. Go back to sleep. The next time you wake up, it'll be morning and everything will be all right.'

'Promise?' His sceptical smile was extremely wry. He might be confused, it told her, but he wasn't stupid. They both knew it was a promise she couldn't make.

The smile dramatically altered his face, softening the taut severity of his features, banishing the grim rigidity that had projected an impression of tightly suppressed hostility and turning him from an object of wary curiosity and compassion into a man of potentially dangerous attractiveness. His face was too lived-in to be classically handsome, but his experience would no doubt add to his charm.

'Things always look clearer in daylight,' she said, resorting to a feeble cliché.

'Clearer but not necessarily better,' he murmured. His hand moved from her waist and emerged from the covers to softly brush her cheekbone. 'It looks like I wasn't the only one who was caught in the wars tonight,' he said. 'You have quite a bump here.'

His touch left a streak of fire on her skin and her fingers flew up to check the tender skin.

'By the way,' Dave had said as he was on his way out the door, 'it's probably a little late to be very effective now, but you should try some ice on that cheek of yours, otherwise you could end up with a beauty of a black eye tomorrow!'

She felt gingerly around the slight puffiness. 'I don't know how it got there. I must have knocked it on something...so much was going on...' she babbled, not wanting to tell Ryan that he had been the one who hurt her.

His fingers lingered along the delicate line of her jaw. 'You have lots of tiny scratches, too.'

'Leaves, a-and twigs...they were blowing around like mad,' she stuttered as his thumb gently skimmed under her lower lip.

'Such smooth, translucent skin. It's a pity to see it marred,' he said, and she wondered if she was crazy to sense a threat in his abstract praise. 'Do they sting?'

If she said yes, would he offer to kiss them better? The thought popped into her head to be savagely squelched.

'No...I—I can't feel them at all,' she said truthfully, trying to master her wayward imagination. Apart from the faint throb on her cheekbone, all she was aware of feeling was the soft friction of his cool finger pads caressing her face, slowly, as if he were a blind man shaping her image in his mind. She shifted her head back on the pillow, escaping the disturbing touch.

There was a tiny pause as their eyes meshed, his intently curious, hers wide with dismay. 'I'm sorry. Am I trespassing on someone else's territory?' he asked gravely, letting his relaxed hand drop to the pillow.

Her green eyes flared with feminist annoyance. 'Yes...mine!'

His gravity turned to sleepy amusement. 'So...you live here all alone?'

In the unlikely event he turned out to be a serial killer, she was telling him nothing he didn't already know. 'Mostly.' Let him make what he liked of that!

'You and the dashing masked hero.'

'Who?' For a moment, she thought his wits had gone wandering again. 'Oh, you mean Zorro? Well, officially he belongs to my landlord, so his legal address is next door, but Ray doesn't seem to mind that he spends most of his time over here.'

'You don't own this place yourself? How do you live? What do you do?'

He mightn't be able to answer questions, but he could certainly ask them! She was tempted to tease him that she was independently wealthy. 'I paint—watercolours, not houses.'

A muscle flicked along the line of his jaw, roughened by a bloom of black stubble. 'You're an artist.'

She watched him turning the idea over in his head.

'Do you sell?'

He obviously had a well-developed mercenary instinct. He could have asked if she was any good. Fortunately, the past nine months had given Nina a sunny confidence in her creative abilities.

She smiled. 'I don't starve.'

His eyes narrowed at her serene response, dipping deliberately to the curving outline of her body, exaggerated by the heaping of covers. 'Exactly how well do you dine?'

Her Mona Lisa smile widened. 'Oh, it's definitely champagne and caviar for breakfast, lunch and dinner around here,' she mocked, 'and that's just for Zorro! I usually plump for truffles with everything, myself.' The smile curled into an open grin as she realised she had made an unintended pun.

'Well, I wouldn't call your proportions exactly Rubenesque,' he concluded in a backhanded compliment, 'so I take it that your truffle boat has actually yet to come in?'

'Something like that. But I'm in no rush. I like the simple life....'

Nearly three years ago, life had been so painfully different. Her widowed grandmother had died after a long, drawn-out battle against the cancer that had gradually eaten away at her indomitable strength and precious joy in life, as well as depriving her of her home and most of her life savings.

After her death, Nina, who had tirelessly nursed her beloved Gran through all the stages of her illness, had been left feeling rootless, her talent burnt out from an endless stream of slick commercial jobs taken to earn a quick buck. She had decided that it was time to spread her wings, to escape the dingy flat in which Gran had dwindled and died, and to travel as she had always dreamed of doing, to seek new experiences that might inspire her to paint again. That decision was the last thing she remembered with any clarity.

Whatever she had done during those two lost years in which she had apparently backpacked around Australasia, she had acquired no lasting souvenirs. But something had eventually drawn her here, to Shearwater Island, where fate had stepped in and she had found herself suddenly at peace.

'I'm happy here.' Her voice carried the lilt of unshakeable conviction. 'Some people say that if they had their

lives to live over again, they'd want things to turn out differently, but I'm glad for everything that's happened in my
life so far because it brought me here!'

His body jerked as if a dagger had struck him square in
the chest, a deep, tearing sound coughing up from his lungs,
the colour draining from his face.

'Ryan?'

He sucked in a hissing breath through clenched teeth.
'It's nothing. I'm all right.'

But it was clearly a lie. Whatever had hit him had hit
him hard. Perspiration glistened on his brow and along his
upper lip, and his eyes were almost white with a soul-
searing pain that dazzled and sickened her.

'Ryan!' He was utterly rigid in the bed and she put her
arms around him and discovered that he was shivering
again. It had happened so fast she was stunned. Was he
lapsing back into shock? 'What's the matter? Is it your
head?'

'No, I'm all right.' His voice was raw with effort.

'No, you're not. For heaven's sake, *tell* me,' she begged,
horrified by the glaze of tears in his eyes and the rictus of
his face as he fought for control. 'This is no time to act all
noble and macho—'

'It's just a cramp!' he ground out, but it was like no
cramp that Nina had ever seen; it seemed to be racking his
whole body. Was he having some kind of a heart attack?

'Are you sure? Can I help?' she pleaded, unable to stand
seeing him in such torment.

'Yes, damn you!' The words ripped from his throat in a
tortured groan of angry self-derision. 'Hold me.' He tore
the barrier of the hot-water bottle from between them and
dragged her against the full length of his shaking body.
'Tight.' Her head arched back as he buried his clammy face
against the curve of her throat, his fierce voice muffled by

her skin. 'Tighter. Hold me, dammit—and for God's sake, don't let go!'

'I won't!' she promised, contracting her arms bruisingly hard across his shuddering back, cupping the nape of his neck with one hand and feeling the opposing bands of rigid muscle writhe beneath his skin. His own arms coiled around her waist like steel ropes, sealing them together like the two halves of a whole, slowly constricting her breathing until she could only take shallow gasps that made red spots dance before her eyes. And still she made no attempt to struggle, for whatever she was suffering was mild in comparison to his elemental pain.

He shuddered soundlessly for long minutes, but even when his rigidity began to ease, Nina didn't dare release him from her fierce embrace. She didn't know if she could give him what he really needed, but she had promised and she wouldn't—*couldn't*—let him down.

Her muscles trembled from the strain and still she held on. His arms slumped over her hips, his body becoming warm, then hot as their combined heat built up within the thick cocoon of blankets, and the ragged, uneven breathing against her throat became a slow and regular sigh of sound, a tempting lullaby seducing her to sleep.

Time became elastic. Her concentration wavered and she closed her eyes to centre her drifting thoughts, and when she opened them a scant few seconds later, it was morning. The cold grey daylight edging in around the imperfectly pulled curtains had chased the shadows from the room.

And from Ryan's face.

For a split second, her sleepy brain registered the pure rightness of waking up beside him, but then her dawning consciousness slammed down the barriers.

They were practically nose-to-nose on the pillow, his warmly exhaled breath ruffling against her soft lips, his spicy male scent a tantalising tang in her nostrils. Their bodies were still melded together, his thigh nestled securely between her crooked legs, her arms tucked like folded wings under his as they loosely encircled each other in warm bands of flesh. With one of her arms caught under his side, Nina was forced to lie there contemplating her mistake.

She had allowed herself to get far too involved. She had allowed her fright, her fears, her compassion, to override her caution and now she was trapped by an unwelcome sense of emotional connection to the stranger she held in her arms.

And not only emotional, she thought, as he stirred in his sleep, his long thigh flexing between her legs, his loins resettling even more intimately into the cradle of her hips. Even through their clothes she could feel the firm contours of his manhood nudging into the cusp of her thigh. An electrical thrill shot through her body, the tips of her breasts suddenly erotically sensitised to the purring vibration of his chest, and she decided that it was definitely time to stage a strategic withdrawal.

She had begun inching her lower arm carefully out from under his body when there was a fluttering under his closed eyelids and a faint frown furrowed his brow, pulling slightly at the neat slash of stitches punctuating his left temple. She stilled, waiting for him to settle back down.

'Nina?' he muttered. He inhaled deeply and his frown was replaced by a sensuous smile of sleepy satisfaction as he identified the unique personal fragrance that spilled across the pillow. 'Nina...'

Eyes still closed, his head dipped and his mouth homed unerringly in on hers, parting her lips in a leisurely kiss that caused a delicious chaos in her startled senses. He made a soft sound of lazy enjoyment as his open mouth moved enticingly back and forth over the succulent plumpness of her lower lip, taking tiny, nibbling bites along the ripe curve before sucking it into his mouth, creating an erotic, rhythmic tugging that made her toes curl inside her socks.

His hand smoothed up her spine to cup the back of her head, holding her still as the moist string of gentle sips deepened to a slow and lingering exploration. His mouth was as smooth as silk, as slick as satin, his tongue gliding over her teeth, licking into the sultry depths of her feminine being, corrupting her with a fierce pleasure that felt both alien and scorchingly familiar.

What had begun as a light, languorous kiss had suddenly flared into white-hot excitement. Nina was bombarded with overwhelming sensations as Ryan swept her along in his hungry passion, the intimate scrape of his beard, the taste of his spicy-warm tongue, the rasp of his ragged breathing and the musky scent of his arousal, all combining to shatter her illusion that she was safe from the wildness that stalked the darkest corridors of her imagination. Ryan's hand slid under her sweatshirt and touched her bare skin, then, almost too late, a shocked awareness of what was about to happen crashed over Nina.

She wrenched herself away from him, burning with shame. 'My God, what are we *doing?*'

'We're doing what comes naturally...making love.'

'I—*no!*' She fought free of the tangled blankets and stumbled out of bed, backing away from him as if he were the devil himself—the devil in a faded sweatshirt with eyes as bright as heaven and a mouth that was pure sin.

'Careful. If you go much farther, you're going to end up in the deep blue sea,' he said, revealing a frightening affinity with her own thoughts that made her wonder what other diabolical talents he possessed.

'I'd better go and see what there is for breakfast,' she mumbled, and fled, deciding that if they were going to eat together, she would make sure that she used a very long spoon!

CHAPTER FOUR

NINA stood behind the wooden-slab breakfast bar overlooking the dining nook and frowned out through the rain-streaked window at the bleak, storm-grey bay. The weather had only marginally improved overnight and high winds still capped the dangerous seas. She didn't need to listen to the marine forecast to know that there would be no ferries running today.

'I guess it would be a misnomer for me to say good morning. It's warm enough in here, but it looks pretty miserable out there, doesn't it?'

The rich, deep voice sent a jolt up her spine and Nina whirled around, her eyes flying wide.

'I'm sorry. Did I startle you?' Ryan said, prowling silently into the kitchen on bare feet, the insincerity of his smile suggesting that he enjoyed catching her off guard.

His all-encompassing look took in her faded stretch jeans and the crisp, white cotton shirt buttoned right up to the collar, a blatant attempt to be prim, which resulted in a tempting provocation. Her hair, tortured into a fat braid, curled over one shoulder, drawing the eye to the soft rise of her breast.

'I hope you don't mind that I grabbed a quick shower and borrowed a razor from your cabinet.'

He passed his hand over his smooth chin, making her remember how his incipient beard had abraded her sensitive skin. She was sullenly resentful of the fact that she hadn't yet had a chance to shower herself; to wash the scent of him from her body. Underneath her fresh clothes she still harboured his lingering touch.

'I see you have my clothes hanging in front of the fire. Do you think they're dry yet?'

'I...' Her voice briefly faltered as she met his challenging gaze, but she managed to suppress the fiery blush that threatened to betray her false composure. She had had plenty of time to pull herself together while the shower was going and she was not about to be flustered into apologising for what had just happened or—more importantly—what had *not* happened in the bedroom. She would just have to pray he was gentleman enough to gloss over the whole embarrassing incident. She busied herself with the coffee-pot to give her an excuse for her restless hands. 'I don't think you'll be able to put them on for at least an hour. I haven't long taken them out of the washing machine and wool takes a while to dry.'

'That was very thoughtful of you. Thank you.'

She could detect no irony in his tone and risked a cautious look under her lashes. He was leaning back against the counter, his sleek head turned towards her, his arms braced against the edge of the rich-grained wood. His expression was relaxed, but the tension in the arc of his back suggested a tightly coiled spring and his eyes were sharply appraising as they darted about the room, barely pausing on Zorro chomping noisily at his bowl. He had pushed the cuffs of the sweatshirt up to his elbows and she could see the deep bruising Dave had mentioned across the back of his forearms.

'I've put out some cereal for you,' she said, indicating the box on the table, 'and there's toast and coffee. You must be hungry—'

'Toast and coffee will do,' he said, making no move to sit down. 'I hope your brother will forgive me wearing his things a little longer,' he continued mildly. 'When is he likely to come back for them?'

'He's not.' Her clipped answer sounded like a snub, so

she softened it with an explanation. 'I mean, Karl doesn't visit very often—only every couple of months or so. The company he works for has started selling a line of surf wear he helped design and it's really taking off, so he's pretty busy right now. He also gets plenty of free samples to wear. I don't think he's likely to miss his old gear so much that he'll make a special trip back for it.'

He turned to face her, propping his hip against the kitchen cabinets. 'Even though the sweater was a gift from you?' he said with a hint of censoriousness.

She shrugged. 'It's not as if I bought it as a sentimental keepsake. I know Karl prefers to keep up with the trends where his clothes are concerned.'

Then the implications of his remark struck her.

'I'm glad we're not going to have to repeat everything we said to you last night,' she said, trying to pitch her words casually, hoping to prompt a spontaneous response. 'You're obviously feeling a lot better this morning. It must be a relief to be clear-headed again. Dave gave me his mobile phone, so if you want to call anyone...' He didn't pick up the hint, so she tried something more obvious. 'I'm sure you must want to be on your way.'

He folded his arms across his chest. 'And which way is that?' he demanded flatly.

The coffeepot clunked against the lip of one of the pottery mugs. 'You don't know?'

He began to shake his head and winced in midmotion.

'But I thought...' She broke off, her nerves jumping.

'What? That because I wanted to make love with you I must therefore be in full command of all my intellectual faculties?' He bared his teeth in a cynical smile. 'I'm sorry to disappoint you, but clarity of mind isn't a prerequisite for sex. Males on the borderline between sleep and waking are usually operating on the most primitive level of human consciousness.

'I float up out of my dreams to find a familiar warm, soft, luscious-smelling woman in my arms who's gloriously responsive to my kisses, it stands to reason I'm not going to be racking my brains for meaningful conversation. All I could think of was that you were available and willing.'

Nina flushed at how easy he made her sound. 'Available doesn't always mean *willing*—'

'Oh, you were willing, right up to the point you got that annoying attack of scruples—'

'*Annoying?*'

'Frustrating, then,' he corrected himself with a shrug that pricked her like a goad.

'You think it would have been more *moral* of me to go ahead and make love with a perfect stranger?' she struck out angrily. 'A man with no name, no personal history? That can be a death sentence these days! You seem to be more concerned about the fact you didn't get any sex this morning than you are about your loss of memory!'

The muscles of his face went tight, his eyes dilating. 'You gave me a name,' he said quietly. 'Ryan.'

Nina's flush became one of shame for letting her temper fly with hurtful words against which she knew he could have no defence. Neither of them looked away as Zorro swiped his last bite and yipped a warning that he was popping out for his morning constitutional.

'I'm sorry—' she began to the accompaniment of the rattling flap on the door.

'You think it doesn't bother me?' Ryan cut her off roughly. 'You think I *like* being this damned helpless? You think I should weak and wailing...sit all alone beweeping my outcast state? And *yes*, by the way, I *do* know that I'm paraphrasing a Shakespearean sonnet. I'm a storehouse of useless information like that! Ask me to quote you sonnets, the names of the planets, the recipe for bearnaise sauce and Einstein's theory of relativity and I'll dazzle you with my breadth of knowledge. I'm full of the whole, damned civilised world—I'm just empty of *me!*' He thumped his chest violently with his clenched fist.

Nina felt a faint, empathetic shudder in the smooth, high, featureless wall that sectioned off a small segment of her life. At least she had the security of knowing that her barrier, invisible yet inexorably solid, was finite. Imagine how she would feel if it stretched into infinity in all directions, preventing her from having any insight into her own personality? She had been wrong to think that Ryan hadn't fully realised the true horror of his situation, wrong to think that he wasn't desperate to regain everything that he had lost. He simply put up a very good front.

She had no right to try to batter it down just because she felt safer viewing him as a victim rather than a man.

'I'm sorry,' she repeated huskily. She finished preparing the coffee on automatic pilot and handed him a steaming mug as a peace offering.

He took it silently and stilled as he looked down into its fragrant contents. Nina followed his brooding gaze and then glanced uneasily at her own bitter black brew as she realised what she had done.

'Don't you take milk and sugar?'

He slowly lifted his eyes to her nervous face. 'I don't know.' He took a cautious sip and his eyebrows rose. 'But apparently, *you* do.' He took a bigger swallow and uttered a sensuous sigh. 'Oh, yes, that tastes good—just how I like it,' he decided, his eyes speculative above the rim. 'Just a lucky guess?'

Nina felt a ridiculous twinge of panic. 'I—it's ideal for shock when it's sweet and milky,' she said, plucking the explanation out of the air without quite knowing why she felt the need to be evasive.

He lifted his mug in an ironic toast. 'It must be pure

serendipity, then, that it happens to be so perfectly to my taste. One sugar, was it?'

'Two.' For some reason, it felt like an admission of guilt, so she hurried on. 'There's white or brown bread for toast,' she offered, determined to avoid a repeat of the awkwardness. 'Which would you prefer?'

He took another savouring sip and smiled guilelessly at her. 'Why don't you surprise me? You've had such good luck so far it almost seems as if you know me better than I know myself.'

'Well, that's not such a difficult accomplishment at the moment, is it?' she shot back, then put a hand over her mouth as if she could push back the words. 'I'm sorry, I shouldn't have said that.'

'Why not? If it's the truth. I can handle the truth, Nina. The question is, can you?'

The air suddenly crackled with electricity, and Nina nearly jumped out of her overly tight skin when there was a sharp rap on the door. She rushed to answer it, gratefully blotting Ryan's cryptic remark out of her mind as she welcomed a dripping Dave Freeman over the threshold.

'Hi, sorry about the early hour, but we have a bit of wind damage that Jeannie wants me to fix up, so I thought I'd nip over and see how the patient is doing before I knuckle down to work,' he said, nodding at Ryan as he eased his muddy gumboots off on the doorstep. 'I also thought I'd take a look up the road before we get any traffic coming through, see if I could find anything.' He slid the black strap off his shoulder and held up the muddy leather travel bag that had been hanging over his back. 'This yours?'

Ryan looked at it impassively. 'I suppose it could be.'

Dave's expression sharpened at the judicious choice of words.

'He still can't remember anything,' Nina confirmed. 'Where did you find the bag?'

'*I* didn't—this little guy did.' Dave jerked his balding head sideways. 'He was dragging it down the road when I met him. From the state of it, I'd say he probably dug it out from the ditch.'

Nina was hard put to distinguish the mud from the dog.

'Oh, Zorro!' The muddy ears drooped at her tone, and she hastened to correct the impression he was in for a scolding. 'Good boy! Clever dog!' His tail started wagging again, thick globules of mud splodging onto the concrete steps, and he danced back out into the rain, obviously intent on garnering more praise for diligent treasure hunting.

Dave had dropped the sodden bag on the kitchen floor and now sat Ryan at the dining-room table to conduct a brief examination. He checked that the sutures were holding satisfactorily and confirmed his previous opinion that there were no signs of delayed concussion or organic damage. Then he accepted Nina's offer of coffee and joined them at the table, directing a series of questions, both pertinent and seemingly pointless, at Ryan.

'Why don't we just look in the bag?' Nina asked impatiently, watching Ryan become increasingly taciturn, frustrated as he was by his inability to answer.

'I just wanted to see how much he could recall in the absence of any retrieval cues. It's almost a textbook presentation of traumatic amnesia,' he told Ryan matter-of-factly. 'Your implicit memories, that is, your learned skills, are intact. It's your event memory that's affected, and of course that encompasses your personal and emotional experiences.'

'Gee, you mean I failed your exam, Doc?' Ryan drawled, mocking his lecturing tone.

Dave took no offence. 'There's no pass or fail. Here, sign your full name for me.' Pushing a spiral notebook across the table, he took out a pen from his shirt pocket and tossed it to Ryan, who, taken by surprise, still caught it easily but hesitated as soon as he touched pen to paper. 'No? Try writing "Ryan",' Dave instructed and they watched as the letters traced smoothly off the end of the pen.

'What does that prove?' Nina asked impatiently. 'You *told* him what to write.'

Dave grinned. 'It proves that he's naturally right-handed.' He shrugged as they both stared at him. 'The direct way isn't always the best way to find pathways through the memory. While Ryan was concentrating on my question rather than on having to choose which hand to catch the pen or to write with, his response flowed naturally. His anxiety reflex wasn't getting in the way. Now, if I'd simply *asked* him whether he was right-or left-handed, he mightn't have been able to tell me.'

Just as Ryan hadn't known how he liked his coffee—until he had tasted it, Nina thought.

'But surely writing is a *learned* skill, and you said all his were intact,' she argued.

'Actually, most of our memory of ourselves involves some kind of learning process. Names, faces, personal experiences...something enters our short-term memory and if it does so with sufficient emotional impact, or we mentally rehearse it often enough by thinking or talking about it, it's passed into permanent storage. Otherwise, it's like writing in smoke on the wind.'

Nina didn't want to hear any more. This wasn't her problem, she told herself.

'You said last night that this would only last a few hours!' she protested.

'I said it was probably temporary,' he said. 'And I still stand by that, but in some people the recovery comes in fragmentary bits and pieces over a period of time, rather like putting together a jigsaw puzzle, instead of conveniently all at once. Do you want to take a look in that bag now?' he asked Ryan.

'Sure,' Ryan said, and got up slowly. Nina made a quick movement to follow but subsided at a discreet signal from Dave, warning her to give the man some space. She forced herself to pick up her half-finished mug of coffee and chat with Dave about the storm, all the while acutely attuned to the sounds from the kitchen.

Ryan crouched down on the floor to unzip the bag, his dark head disappearing below the line of the counter.

When he rose a few minutes later, Nina broke off her conversation and bounced up out of her chair. 'Well? What's in it?' she demanded.

He shrugged. 'Everything's pretty wet, but…a few toiletries, some clothes, shoes—'

'A weekend bag,' she affirmed, impatient with his vagueness. 'But is it *yours?*'

'The clothes appear to be about the right size…'

Her heart zoomed into her sneakers. '*Appear* to be? So you don't recognise anything?'

'No, but then, I don't have to when I have this.' Ryan tossed a damp leather billfold onto the counter.

It fell open with a squelch, revealing a driver's licence in the clear plastic window. The dark face stared up at her from the digitised photograph, and she quickly shifted her gaze from the icy blue eyes to the name printed beside the miniaturised image. '"Ryan Flint".' She lifted her head to gauge his reaction.

None was visible. His expression was impassive, waiting…

'Ryan *Liam* Flint.' He added the name she hadn't bothered to read.

She ignored his correction, her eyes as transparent as green glass, as neutral as his own. 'We were right about the cigarette lighter being yours, then.'

He held himself very still. 'So it would seem.'

'No credit cards, no business cards, very little money—' Nina was shamelessly checking the rest of the billfold '—one stub of a return ferry ticket from Auckland. You seem to be travelling incredibly light for a man who must have paid a small fortune for his clothes.'

'Perhaps that's why,' he said.

The fine tension that had spun out during their oddly detached exchange snapped when Dave stood up and held out his hand across the bench. 'Hi, I'm pleased to meet you. I'm Dave Freeman.'

'I'm Ryan Flint.' The ice-blue eyes glinted with wry appreciation as he completed the polite ritual and the two men shook hands.

'How do you feel about being able to say that?' Dave asked.

Ryan smiled thinly at him. 'Relieved that I finally have a peg on which to hang myself.'

'I hope you don't mean that literally!'

The smile became one of amused confidence. 'I don't think I'm the suicidal type.'

Dave stroked his silver beard thoughtfully. 'What type of man do you think you are?'

The curve of Ryan's mouth flattened. 'Not a quitter. I don't quit until I get what I want.'

Nina's fingers tightened on the edges of the billfold.

'That's a strong statement,' Dave mused. 'It sounds as if it comes from the heart.'

'What makes you so sure I have one?' Ryan lifted one cynical brow.

'I just took your pulse, remember?' Dave grinned. 'Your resting heart rate is slightly high, but considering your injuries I'd say you're an extremely fit young man.'

'You're thirty-three,' Nina said, having done mental calculations from the birth date on the licence.

Ryan ran his fingers through his hair, pushing it back off his injured forehead. 'Not so young, then. Old enough to know that there may be things that I don't *want* to remember about myself.'

Nina stiffened, but neither man was looking at her.

'A pity they don't include addresses on those things,' Dave said, nodding towards the licence. 'But at least now you have a name and some sort of sense of your own character.

'We could notify the police, but you might want to wait a little before you declare yourself an official missing person. Maybe it's a good thing that this storm hasn't passed over yet. A couple more days of unstressed peace and quiet could be all you need to fully recover, or at least get to the point where you can slot back into your normal life without any major hassles,' he added with the shrewd foresight of a man who was used to juggling the needs of wealthy patients anxious to avoid drawing public notice to their very private problems.

'You mean cross my fingers and hope for the best!' Ryan translated cynically.

'If you like. It's your call.'

Ryan looked struck by the idea that he was still in control of his destiny. 'In that case, you're right,' he admitted. 'Wait and see sounds a far preferable strategy to my walking stone blind into the arms of the system.'

'Okay. So there's no rush, no performance pressure. You don't have to try to force your memories to surface. You can relax and let them lap over to you. You never know, someone around here may recognise you, and in the meantime you couldn't have landed yourself with a more ideal hostess—'

'Wait a minute!' Nina dropped the billfold from nerveless fingers. 'You're not suggesting that he stays on *here!*'

'Why not? You've got the room,' Dave pointed out genially. 'And it's not as if you aren't used to having male boarders.'

'I thought you lived here alone,' Ryan said, frowning.

'I...in the summer, Ray rents out the spare rooms to some of the conservation department workers and volunteers who come to do ecological surveys and study projects at the nature and marine reserves,' she said reluctantly, knowing that with Dave listening she had no choice but to admit the truth.

'They only stay for a few weeks at a time and I don't have to pay Ray any rent while I'm playing landlady.' Most of the workers were young and idealistic, committed to saving the planet, and while Nina had enjoyed the stimulation of their company, she had been happy to wave them off again and return her undivided attention to her work. 'But I'm really only a tenant, too, and while Ray is away, I don't think I should...' She broke off as Dave's salt-and-pepper eyebrows rose in surprise at her apparent hesitation.

'I'm sure he wouldn't mind your putting Ryan up for a few days. Ray's always had a helping hand for strays. In fact, didn't he do the same for you when you arrived on Shearwater in very similar circumstances, hurt and with nowhere to go? Offer you a place to live until you sorted out what you wanted to do—which in your case was to stay on? Is he off at his daughter's? If you're worried about having his permission, why don't you call him there and ask?'

Nina was beaten and she knew it. 'I suppose you're right,' she said weakly. 'It's just that I'm really busy finishing a commission right now—'

Ryan, who had been letting Dave do the persuading, interrupted smoothly. 'I won't interfere with your work. You'll hardly even know I'm here.'

Oh, she would know, Nina thought grimly. She had the

feeling that every moment he was in the house she would be aware of him with every fibre of her being.

'And it's good to know that there's someone on hand with some personal experience of what I'm going through,' he added ominously. 'Maybe you can give me some useful tips on how to cope.'

She went cold all over. 'I don't think so.'

He didn't take the hint. 'I heard you and Dave talking about your amnesia last night. How did it happen?'

Nina suppressed her welling panic. With this interested audience, she knew it wouldn't do to overreact. She would satisfy his curiosity and hope he dropped the subject. 'I fell down a wet companionway coming over here on the ferry and bumped my head on the stair rail,' she clipped, gathering up the coffee mugs from the table. 'Or so I'm told. It's all rather hazy.'

'Were you badly hurt?' His voice was taut with a controlled emotion that she refused to recognise.

'I wasn't hurt at all, just dazed,' she dismissed with a shrug. 'All I got was a small graze on the side of my face— nothing to make a big fuss about—'

'But you still have the amnesia.'

'Look, it's no big deal,' she said impatiently, carrying the mugs over to the sink. 'I was a footloose traveller and had all my worldly goods in a backpack. I'd obviously intended to stay on Shearwater for a while, so there was no urgency for me to get back to wherever I'd been before, especially when I discovered how much I enjoyed living here.'

Her green eyes suddenly lit with humour. 'You might even say it was preordained because the ferry company was so relieved that I wasn't interested in suing that they gave me a big fat cheque by way of apology, which I used to pay Ray for my first few months rent in advance. Then I started painting and never looked back. So you see, everything actually worked out perfectly for me in the end!'

She turned her back on his dubious expression and concentrated on washing out the mugs with overly meticulous care.

Behind her she heard Dave draw Ryan aside for some low-voiced counsel about his condition, and then he announced he should be getting back to his whip-cracking wife.

Nina quickly dried her dripping hands on a tea-towel. 'I guess you'd better have your cell phone back,' she said, handing it to him from the bench.

'Maybe it's time you talked Ray into having a phone line put in here,' he commented, slipping it into the hip pocket of his trousers.

She shook her head. 'It's much more peaceful without. I like not being available to all and sundry at the push of a button. People think twice about interrupting you if they have to make the effort to do it in person!'

'That's definitely my cue to leave!' Dave chuckled. 'Well, good luck, Ryan.' He clapped him on the arm. 'Let me know how you get on. I'm in the green house at the end if you need anything else, and Jeannie and I are going back to Auckland the day after tomorrow, weather permitting, if you want company on your way back to civilisation.'

'Thanks for the offer.'

'Uh, are you sure you don't want another cup of coffee?' Nina blurted, suddenly loath to see him go. Nervous as he made her, she was much more nervous about being alone with her disturbing guest.

'I think she's afraid that I'm going to grow fangs as soon as your back's turned,' Ryan said with uncanny perception.

'You could be a serial killer for all we know about you,' she pointed out nastily.

Dave scratched his head. 'Well, based on many years of experience observing what we in the psychiatric profession refer to as "total wackos", I can honestly say that I don't think that Ryan is one of them.'

'"*Total wackos*"?' Nina echoed faintly.

He grinned. 'It's a clinical term—I guess you'd need seven years of medical school to understand it. To put it in layman's terms, Ryan shows no signs of a psychotic personality.'

Ryan was grinning now, too, and Nina's feathers were thoroughly ruffled by the male conspiracy.

'He might just be very good at hiding it,' she said tartly.

'That's true. So what do you want me to do?' The question was sober, but the glint in his eye was definitely amused. He seemed to guess that she didn't seriously view Ryan as a physical threat.

She was not going to play head games with someone who was way overqualified to tie her up in embarrassing knots. Who knew what inner secrets she might be tricked into revealing? God, what if she found herself telling him that she and Ryan had already crossed the line between hostess and guest?

As her face burned with guilt, she saw Dave's speculative gaze suddenly shift to Ryan, who unfortunately was wearing a glaringly obvious poker face.

'Oh…go home to your wife!' Nina said in exasperation, waving him towards the door.

'Right!' Dave said cheerfully, picking up his coat. 'Uh-oh, sorry…' As he opened the door, Zorro had shot in between his legs on mud-soaked paws.

'Hey, where do you think you're going, mate!' Nina's heart flipped at the hint of Australian drawl, and Zorro screeched to a halt as Ryan stooped and cupped his furry face in his elegant hands to look into his eyes and deliver a stern lecture on consideration for others. 'You don't get to run around in here until we've got you cleaned up,' he finished.

Unoffended by the reprimand, Zorro stretched up on his hind legs to try to lick the nose that had just poked itself into his business, a tribute to the new dominant male of the household. Ryan laughed, a rich, vibrant sound of pure enjoyment that made Nina's heart flip again. Laughing, he was another man entirely—warm and appealing rather than cool and brooding. Looking at him was like peering down a kaleidoscope, each shake of his personality presenting a different arrangement of the disconnected fragments of his life.

'You know how to handle dogs,' Dave said from the stoop, fighting the wind to get his arms into his coat. 'Have you got one yourself?'

'No, but—' Ryan lifted his head, his eyes shimmering '—but I did have one as a child,' he said slowly. 'A big white dog with lots of spots…like in that Disney movie.' His words were unconsciously boyish. 'He was a Dalmatian.'

'Do you remember his name?'

Ryan thought, then shook his head.

'Spot?' Nina suggested facetiously.

He shot her a scathing look. 'I should hope that I was a bit more creative than that!' He glanced back down at Zorro, his frown suggesting he was struggling to expand the picture in his mind. 'There was a big yard…and a tree—the dog used to sit in the shade and the leaves' shadows would look like more spots. But…no…' He let out a puff of frustration. 'I can't remember any more.'

'That's the way things usually start coming back,' Dave encouraged, flicking up his hood against the rain. 'Distant recollections pop into your mind first, then progressively more recent memories begin to appear. I told you it would happen!' He went off, smug in the knowledge that his professional reputation was still intact.

Nina shut the door behind him and took a deep breath as she turned to face her unwelcome duty, only to have the wind sucked out of her sails.

'I know you're busy, so if you want to go off and paint or whatever, I'll wash this grubby wretch for you.' Ryan ruffled Zorro's head affectionately, not seeming to care about the amount of dirt he was getting on his hands. 'And once I've cleaned up that bag of mine—' he jerked his head towards the limp mound of expensive leather '—I can give this floor a good mopping.'

Even though he was dressed in Karl's sloppy clothes, Nina found it hard to picture Ryan Flint doing mundane domestic chores. There was a kind of natural arrogance about him that made it easier to visualise him paying someone *else* to do his cleaning.

'Oh, you don't have to do that...' she began awkwardly.

He rose, holding out his flat hand to instruct a quivering Zorro to sit and stay, which—miraculously—he did!

'I may have lost my memory, but I'm not helpless,' he said firmly. 'I know I've been foisted on you and I don't intend to be a burden. I want to make myself useful, not just lie around brooding over my problems. Please—go ahead with your work and forget that I'm here.'

Faced with such a graceful offer, what could Nina do but grudgingly accept? However, just as she had expected, it was easier said than done, and over the next two days, cooped up inside with him by the continuing bad weather, Nina felt more and more like a prisoner in her own home, the boundaries of her personal space shrinking with each successive encounter with her unsettling guest.

Even tucked away in her studio with the door firmly shut, radio going and the wind providing sufficient ambient noise to block out anything that was happening in the rest of the house, she found that she couldn't summon the tightly focused concentration she needed for sustained close work.

So while George's plants languished on her drawing board, she turned to practising some sky studies, creating free adaptations from the sketches she had made the last time she had walked on the beach, early on the morning of the storm, when striking formations of clouds were building up against the horizon, the rising wind tugging at the pages of her sketchbook as she raced to capture pencilled snapshots of the rapidly changing scene.

She worked quickly as she painted, keeping the paper damp so that the edges of the clouds melted into one another, their varying tones building in intensity where the colours overlaid one another. The longer she worked on that first day, the more relaxed she became, and she might have eventually succeeded in her aim of pushing Ryan Flint right out of her mind if he hadn't come knocking on her studio door.

'I hope it's okay that I helped myself to some lunch. I thought you might be hungry by now, too,' he said, handing her a piled plate as he sauntered past. 'So this is where you work. Would you mind if I had a look around?'

Since he was already doing so, his polite question was rather redundant, but Nina *had* minded, and the delicious grilled cheese-and-tomato sandwiches were not enough of a bribe to prevent her from firmly telling him that her studio was off-limits to visitors. She didn't like the expression of curious absorption on his face as he roamed the room, studying the orderly clutter. Even when he pronounced himself fascinated by the contrast between her botanical drawings and the moody seascapes lining the walls, she felt no pleasure in his praise, only a knotted tension in her stomach that didn't go away until she had shooed him out of the studio.

'I think I know about this,' he said quietly as she hustled him out the door. 'It feels familiar....'

'Really? Good for you,' she said, in no mood to deal with another of his spooky forays into the distant past. She was an artist, not a therapist, she told him.

But out of sight was not out of mind, and although she tried to keep their contact to a minimum, she was haunted by a passionate awareness that with every word, every look, every touch, he was drawing her closer to the brink of a dangerous abyss.

When she woke on the third morning to the weak rays of the sun and the raucous cries of gulls reclaiming their scavenging rights on the beach, Nina felt a sharp sense of anticlimax.

The air was still. The storm was over. The danger was past. She hadn't given in to her treacherous desires. Today Ryan Flint would be out of her life forever.

CHAPTER FIVE

'RYAN? *Ryan?*' Nina moved through the house, her voice bouncing emptily off the painted walls.

When she had had her shower, the walls were still dewy, the small cake of guest soap she had put out still covered with remnants of foam, so she had assumed that Ryan was already up and about, probably getting breakfast for both of them as he had insisted on doing the previous morning.

But there was no sign of Ryan in the living area and her heart began to thump uncomfortably fast as she hurried back up the hall.

Last night, when she had tried to bring up the subject of his leaving, Ryan had said he was tired and wanted an early night, but even though she had mentioned that if the ferries were sailing there would be an early commuter run, surely he wouldn't have left without saying goodbye!

She cautiously opened the door to his room, her jaw relaxing when she saw the black leather bag sitting under the neatly made bed.

Her eyes swept around the pristine room. Ryan was still only experiencing vague flashes of recall, but obviously the habit of personal tidiness was too deeply ingrained to be ignored. It might simply be that he was consciously on his best behaviour, but she was inclined to think that perhaps Ryan Flint was a domesticated animal after all.

Not necessarily tamed, just domesticated. Perhaps even *married.* She had used that unpalatable thought to help her dam the cascade of little thrills that had flooded through her whenever she turned and caught Ryan unexpectedly watching her with that sexy narrowing of his eyes.

Retracing her steps to the living room, Nina saw that the fire had been restoked and suddenly realised that Zorro, too, was missing. For the past couple of days, with Nina doing her best to make herself inaccessible, man and dog had been inseparable companions.

Perhaps they'd gone for a walk along the beach. Maybe Ryan had wanted to see if anyone would recognise him or vice versa, or perhaps he had wanted to call in on Dave Freeman to ask for a lift over to the jetty.

Nina grabbed the elderly binoculars from the bookcase and pushed open the sliding door, then stood on the deck to scan the beach, her body soaking up the weak rays of sunshine, which didn't quite compensate for the chilly sea breeze lifting the loose hair off her shoulders and knifing keenly through her hand-knitted green jumper.

There were only three people visible on the right, two of them scrambling over a yacht that had been blown from its mooring up onto the beach. The other figure was so tall and skeletally thin it had to be Chas Peterson, dipping and bending as he dragged a large sack along the snaking high-waterline, collecting seaweed to feed the voracious compost heap that fertilised his highly prized vegetable garden.

In the other direction, on the short, triangular section of beach where the creek that ran down the rocky, scrub-covered hill flattened out to meet the sea, a large black Labrador was chasing seagulls away from a lump on the wet sand, while two children prodded ghoulishly with sticks at the obviously fishy corpse.

As Nina lowered the binoculars, she caught a glimpse of movement next door, a grey head moving off around the side of the house.

Ray Stewart was home again.

That meant the ferries were definitely back on schedule.

Normally, she would have gone straight over to say a cheery hello and listen to all Ray's news about his family and fill him in on anything interesting that had occurred while he was away, but this morning she slunk back inside the house, guiltily aware that she was only putting off the inevitable.

She knew Ray would be annoyed that he had missed the drama of Ryan's arrival and would want to share in the vicarious excitement by peppering her with questions about her mysterious guest. Nina had too many unanswered questions herself. She didn't want to probe too deeply into her reactions to Ryan or think too hard about the dichotomy of her feelings—the compulsion to keep him at arm's length that warred with the powerful undercurrent of attraction.

She ate her solitary breakfast and cleared away the dishes, then flitted around the living room tidying up, pausing frequently to glance out the window.

As she straightened the cover on the couch, she remembered Zorro making a nuisance of himself last night, snuffling and pawing at the fabric tucked deep into the crease where the padded back met the sagging seat. At the time, she had suspected him of having buried one of his bones down there, but a cursory inspection had produced nothing except fluff. Rather an embarrassing quantity of fluff! She couldn't remember the last time she had thoroughly vacuumed the couch, and now, looking closely at the floral pattern, she could see faint streaks of dried mud on the bottom of the throw where Ryan's feet had lain that first night. Maybe it was time to put the whole thing in the washing machine.

The thick woven cotton was quite tightly wedged into the crease and Nina had to tug hard to get the crumpled folds to emerge, staggering back as the cover finally sprang free, bringing with it a small, dark object that bounced onto the floor.

When she picked it up, she discovered she was looking at a polished black leather card case with a tiny gold catch.

She popped it open. Tucked behind a leather strip in the lid was a platinum credit card bearing the name of Ryan Flint...no, not one, but *two* platinum credit cards, two bank smart cards and an unmarked magnetic swipe card that was obviously some kind of security key.

Nina's gaze fell to the bottom of the case, and she lifted out one of the thick, pale cream cards embossed with stark black lettering.

Ryan Flint
Pacific Rim Galleries
Honolulu, Sydney, Melbourne, Auckland

Nina's eyes widened, her body going rigid, her hand clenching around the card, the sharp corners digging into her damp palm. Sweat bloomed across her body and she suddenly found her breathing locked into a frightening rhythm of shallow, uneven gasps, acid searing the back of her tongue. She slumped down on the couch, fighting for oxygen, retaining just enough presence of mind to push her head down between her denim-clad knees.

Ryan Flint.

Pacific Rim Galleries.

Blackness hazed the edge of her vision and she fought to push the encroaching nightmare back. The blood pounded in her skull and gradually the suffocating tightness in her chest eased enough for her to suck in a deep, reviving breath. Blindly, she pushed the little leather case back where she had found it, forcing it deep out of sight, and blundered for the door.

She ran across the springy grass between the two houses, stumbling as she mounted Ray's uneven wooden steps, her head bobbing unevenly on her shoulders as she looked around for the old man, unable to make herself call out. Her throat felt swollen, grated raw, and she had no saliva to help her swallow. There was a pain in her hand and she looked down, surprised to see her fist still tightly clenched. It took a monumental effort to force her fingers to unfold and she stared at the mangled card in the centre of her palm.

The peeling front door stood open as it usually did when Ray was home and Nina walked inside on stiff legs, not stopping until she had reached the kitchen and the battered grey telephone fixed to the wall next to a corkboard smothered in children's crayoned drawings and letters.

As if she were standing outside herself, Nina watched her hand reach out and unhook the receiver. Smoothing out the card on the chipped Formica bench with her other hand, she stared at it with glassy green eyes.

Ryan Flint. Pacific Rim Galleries.

She began to punch in the telephone number, not even registering the fact that the number she was dialling was several digits different from that printed on the corner of the card.

'Good morning. Pacific Rim Galleries. Ryan Flint's office. May I help you?'

The professional trill sent a shudder down Nina's spine and she swayed, almost dropping the receiver.

'No…that is, I…' Nina struggled to overcome the numbing of her tongue.

'I'm sorry. This is Mr Flint's private line. Did you want the main gallery?'

Nina moistened her bloodless lips. 'I—could I speak to Ryan, please,' she said in a dry husk completely unlike her usual cool, clear tone.

'I'm afraid Mr Flint isn't here at the moment. Can I put you through to his personal assistant?'

'Uh…no. When will he be back?'

'Not for at least two weeks, I'm afraid. Mr Flint is on holiday.'

'Oh…well, perhaps I'll call him at home, then.'

'I'm afraid I can't give you that number. It's unlisted—'
'I know.'

The bright professional voice became a little more friendly and confiding. 'I'm afraid you won't get hold of him at home for the next couple of weeks, either. I understand he was going away and didn't want to be disturbed. He did say he would check messages on his mobile, although currently it appears to be switched off.'

More likely buried in mud at the bottom of a ditch, Nina thought with a mirthless smile.

'In case you don't get in touch with him, would you like me to tell him you called? If you'd just give me your name—'

Nina quietly hung up. And then she began to shake. Wrapping her arms around her waist, she leaned her shuddering body against the bench for support as the memory of the two months immediately following her grandmother's death suddenly emerged from the blank wall in her mind, crystallising into images so bright and sharp that she found it hard to believe that she hadn't been able to summon them before.

But then, she hadn't summoned them this time, either. They had ambushed her when she least expected it, hitting her with the force of an avalanche and sweeping away all the smug certainties that she had nurtured in the past nine months. Memories that she had thought were lost forever, severed from her experience and locked away in an inaccessible part of her brain, had found an escape portal.

Ryan Flint.

...The starkly beautiful gallery in a renovated church a short stroll from Auckland's Albert Park, where Nina used to lunch alfresco when she was working in the city. The gallery she used to visit and in which she innocently fantasised her paintings might one day hang!

…The elegant city restaurant where there had been such a ghastly scene.

…The fateful party in the elegant Parnell house where Ryan had shredded her pride and she had slapped his arrogant face.

What miserable freak of fate had brought Ryan Flint back into her unknowing orbit? Ryan Flint, the former professional gambler who—according to Karl—had won a rundown Sydney art gallery in a high-rolling poker game when he was twenty-six and parlayed it into a string of prestigious galleries that had made him into a multimillionaire and serious art collector in his own right.

The bastard!

The rage erupted in her veins.

No wonder she had found his presence obscurely threatening! No *wonder* she had instinctively erected such strong mental barriers against him.

She remembered the shock she had felt when she first touched him out in the storm. Although she had shrugged it off at the time, it had obviously been a shock of physical recognition; only her mind had refused to acknowledge what her senses were telling her.

Of *course* she knew who he was. He was the unprincipled swine who had nearly ruined Karl's life!

The stormy emotions that Nina had felt at the time came back in a devastating rush.

She hadn't taken off on her travels straight after her grandmother's funeral as she had hazily assumed. She had decided to stay on in Auckland until the lease on the flat had officially run out, working out her notice at the commercial art firm and saving every cent she could for her planned trip. For the first time in three years, Nina had been able to look towards a cloudless future.

Then Karl had entangled her in his disastrous romance. A few days after her grandmother's funeral, he had introduced her to Ryan Flint in the hope that she would influence him to look favourably on Karl's desire to marry his sister.

Karl had been dating Katy Flint for several months—secretly, because wealthy Big Brother didn't approve of his pretty nineteen-year-old sister hanging around with a long-haired, chain-smoking, antiauthoritarian drop-out who spent most of his time surfing and the rest of it living suspiciously well on unspecified odd jobs that he picked up from amongst his dubious set of friends.

Nina, who had never felt comfortable with her foster-brother's previous free-and-easy attitude to drugs and selfish avoidance of any sort of responsibility, had been in secret sympathy with Big Brother's protective instincts…until she had actually met him!

Sparks had flown immediately, Ryan tarring her with the same brush as her brother and Nina loyally refusing to admit that she, too, doubted Karl's suitability for marriage—especially to a gentle-natured girl like Katy.

Karl had revelled in the role of star-crossed lover, but only because his youthful arrogance could not conceive of his beloved actually choosing her brother over him. In any event, he had grossly underestimated Ryan's ruthless determination to smash up the relationship. It had all ended very messily, with Karl arrested on a cannabis charge and Katy dumping him when he tried to blame her brother for setting him up.

Nina's last memory of Ryan was the triumphant smile on his face as he had taken a furious punch on the jaw from Karl outside the courthouse, while at his side, Katy had screamed at her erstwhile lover to stop.

It came as no surprise to realise that Karl might have had his own reasons for so philosophically accepting Nina's loss of memory for a period that might well have included a stint in prison for him.

Was that why he had taken so long to respond to the first postcard she had sent him a couple of months after her arrival on Shearwater? He had said it was because he was travelling so much in his new job, but perhaps it was because he was ashamed of what had happened and welcomed the chance of a clean slate. Certainly, he was much less reckless and more disciplined than the hot-headed twenty-year-old she had remembered him to be.

The sound of voices and footsteps on the creaking planks of the front veranda had Nina straightening up, snatching the creased business card off the counter and stuffing it into the pocket of her jeans.

She hastened back to the front door, stepping out into a patch of sunlight that momentarily dazzled her vision.

'Hi, Ray, I...'

She stopped, raising her hand to shade her eyes as she saw the dark outline of his much taller companion. Her pupils contracted to pinpoints as she took in the pleasant expression on the lean, smiling face.

'I guess today I'm allowed to greet you with a "good morning",' Ryan said as Zorro trotted forward to sniff at her laces.

Nina's head whirled. She had no idea how to react. Should she just blurt out that she had finally recognised who he was?

'You came racing over here for nothing,' Ray cackled. 'Ryan's already beaten you to it!'

'*What?*' Nina's gaze zigzagged violently between the two men. Had Ryan now remembered the rest? So far, all he had managed to dredge up were fragments of his childhood.

'Saw him walking along the beach with Zorro, so I called him in. He told me all about your rescue effort,' Ray expanded, shuffling over to the bench seat against the blistered weatherboards and lowering himself stiffly onto it with an audible creak of his arthritic bones. He sighed with relief, his knobbly hand resting the smooth kauri walking-stick against his spindly knee.

'Cooked up some bacon and eggs for me, too, while we had our chat. Almost as good as yours! I was glad to hear you had a bit of company—I worried about you in that big blow. Thought I might come back to find you picking through a pile of matchwood, the way they were talking about it on the TV!'

'It wasn't *that* bad here...' Nina began, instinctively playing down her fear.

'Bad enough, according to the fishermen I met on the wharf,' Ray muttered gruffly, a scowl crossing his whiskery, weather-beaten face. 'And I can see it around here. Some of my roofing iron around back is flapping loose and I've sprung a few weatherboards. No use thinking I'll ever get round to fixing it, not with these hands the way they are.' He held up the gnarled fingers, distorted by the disease in his joints. An ex-fisherman, he had spent most of his working life in the open, and now he chafed at the fact that his hardy, work-toughened body was letting him down. 'I've been thinking it's about time this place had a general spruce-up anyway....'

'Perhaps you'd better see if you can get Bill Sawyer to come and take a look—'

'And get charged an arm and a leg for knocking in a few nails? No thanks!' Ray was generous in many respects, but he hated spending an unnecessary dollar. 'Not when I have Ryan here offering to do it for nothing but a shared crust and a roof over his head.'

'*Ryan!*' Nina's chin jerked around. Sitting on the wide veranda rail, his arms propped on the cracked wood on either side of his hips, he looked amused at her stunned reaction. In the pale ivory trousers and indigo cashmere sweater, which were among the clothes he'd had to wash from his bag, he was infuriatingly attractive, and his cocky grin seemed to imply he knew it.

'Yep. He's gonna be my handyman for the next few days,' Ray said. 'So you'll have your temporary tenant for a bit longer. Naturally, I'll adjust your rent since he's gonna need meals—'

'*Handyman!* But—you can't do that! He can't stay here,' Nina squawked. 'He has to get back!'

'To what?' Ryan slammed the ball back into her court with effortless ease. 'Freeman was right. Without any outside pressure, my memory's coming back...just a bit more slowly than he predicted. I don't want to mess with the process. Maybe I was travelling light for a reason—the same reason I was only carrying a few dollars. Maybe I'm in some sort of trouble. I don't want to go back to a life I don't remember. I'd be too vulnerable. Surely *you* can identify with that.'

Nina's mouth opened and closed soundlessly.

'He's got you there, girl,' Ray said slyly.

It was on the tip of her tongue to say that a man with two platinum credit cards would *never* be as vulnerable as a roving artist with scarcely an asset to her name. But something held her back.

'For goodness' sake, it's ridiculous!' she said hotly. 'What makes you think he'll be any good at doing repairs? I doubt if he even knows which end of a hammer is which.'

Ryan's head tilted, his hair gleaming blue-black in the sun. 'What makes you say that?'

She spun around and grabbed up his hands, turning them over to display the palms. 'Well, look! You're obviously not used to manual labour. No-one who works with tools has hands *this* soft,' she jeered, drawing her fingers across his smooth skin. 'And your fingernails have been *manicured.*'

He looked down at her, standing between his splayed

knees, a willing captive to her strong artist's grip. 'I thought women liked a man to have nice hands,' he murmured smokily. 'You have such silken skin yourselves it seems a shame to risk damaging it with rough handling.'

Nina snatched her fingers away. It had been a big mistake to touch him. He might have lost his memory, but he hadn't lost his instinctive ability to flirt or the basic sensuality of his nature.

Even when they had been snapping and snarling at each other over their respective siblings, Ryan had somehow managed to inject an element of sexual provocation into their encounters. To her horror, Nina had started to feel a kick of guilty excitement every time she saw him and had secretly thrilled to the smouldering blue fire that had flared in his eyes whenever she scored a point in one of their close verbal jousts.

Unlike her, Ryan had not attempted to hide the fact that he was aroused by her spirited opposition to his entrenched ideas. His girlfriend of the time had been a gorgeous, slinky blond creature who Nina had cattily decided looked as if she had never opposed an idea from a man in her life!

'Maybe you're a hairdresser. They always have soft, pampered hands,' she suggested evilly.

To her dismay, he took that as an invitation to cup her slender neck, his thumbs resting in the sensitive spot just below her ears, and combed his fingers experimentally up through the hair at the nape of her neck.

'I must admit, doing this does *feel* familiar,' he mused, openly goading. 'Perhaps if you let me wash it for you tonight, it might give me a better clue.'

Since Nina always washed her hair in the shower, the suggestion made her flinch. She hurriedly stepped back out of reach, an irresistible vision arising in her mind of Ryan standing behind her under the flow of water, slowly massaging her soapy scalp.

Her lashes flicked up and she was mortified to find him studying her hot cheeks with knowing eyes. 'Inspiring thoughts?' he asked blandly.

She remembered how clever he was with words. His technique for vanquishing Karl had included treating the younger man with an unpredictable mixture of polite condescension and thinly veiled contempt, deliberately goading him into outbursts of temper that only succeeded in making him sound like a petulant boy.

'I don't need a qualified master builder to do the job,' Ray was saying testily. 'I'm only a fisherman and I still managed to build most of this place myself. Acourse, it took a good few years....'

'That's not really the point,' she told him, attempting to outstare her tormentor as she directed another question at him. 'What if someone's already worried about you? What about your family?' she challenged.

His parents had lived somewhere in Europe, but what about Katy? Had she graduated with her commerce degree and gone on to postgraduate study at Harvard as Ryan had originally planned?

'What if you're married?' she added, watching with grim satisfaction as his face become carved out of stone.

Three years ago, he had been a confirmed bachelor. The slinky blonde had been only one of a parade of women through his life. Katy had confided that she had never known her brother to fall in love.

'Women are always claiming to be in love with him. They all make it too easy for him,' she had complained to Nina, trying to explain why Ryan was incapable of understanding the very special love that she and Karl shared. 'He's such a cynic I don't think he'll ever get married except for practical reasons—like, you know, buffing up his family image.'

'You *could* be married,' she repeated vengefully.

A dark shadow moved behind the pale eyes. 'So could you,' he quietly pointed out.

'*Me?*'

'Who's to say that in those two years you say that you can't remember, that *you* didn't get married?'

She was furious at him for turning the tables, nauseated by the suggestion. 'Don't be ridiculous. Of course I didn't. Karl would have told me!' she snapped. 'I'm hardly likely to have got married without letting my brother know—'

'*Foster*-brother—'

'Whatever!' She shrugged angrily. 'Even if it happened while I was in the middle of the Aussie outback, I would have at least sent him a postcard about it.' Karl had vaguely mentioned getting a few postcards from her while she was away, but he wasn't one for filing his correspondence and she had never bothered to ask him where they had come from or what they said. If it had been important, he would have told her. 'Besides, I wasn't wearing a wedding ring when I arrived.'

Ryan raised his splayed hands. 'Neither was I.'

'Some men don't!'

He smiled cynically. 'Some women don't, either.'

He'd know all about that! she thought snidely. Katy had said that not all the women who threw themselves at his head were single, although the ones he deigned to catch were invariably unattached.

'If I were married, I'd wear a ring,' she announced definitively, hands on her hips.

He stood up, towering over her, adopting an identical stance. 'So would I.'

Stalemate! He wasn't going to be pressured, or persuaded by appeals to his nonexistent conscience, into leaving Shearwater Island until he was good and ready to go.

For God's sake, why couldn't he see there was nothing for him here? And now she was in the invidious position of holding the key to his identity when the last thing she wanted to do was *help* him. Why should she humiliate herself by revealing the circumstances of their brief acquaintanceship? She had every right to despise him. What he had done to Karl was unforgivable!

'Look at you two!' Ray chuckled, his white hair fluffed up into a halo by the breeze. 'You look as if you're about to put up your dukes! I would've thought you'd have been dead keen on the idea, Nina. You've been after me for months to get some maintenance done—those warped front steps of mine, for instance. And after Ryan's finished here, maybe I can get him to give your roof a bit of a going-over. I noticed there's a patch or two of rust starting to show up....'

This sounded as if it was turning into a long-term position, Nina thought, aghast. 'I don't think you should risk using someone who doesn't know exactly what they're doing up there,' she muttered. 'He'll probably fall off and break his neck!'

'Is that concern for me, or wishful thinking?' Ryan asked sardonically. 'Ray's shown me what needs doing and I'm willing to have a go. You've told me that a lot of people around here work a barter system—that's what I'm doing. It seems a fair exchange of favours to me. Or do you think that I'm going to exploit the trust of a helpless old man for some nefarious purpose of my own?'

'Hey, less of the "helpless" there, Sonny Jim!' Ray barked, rapping his stick on the hollow boards, demonstrating that his hearing was still as sharp as his comprehension. 'I may look like a decrepit old wreck, but I'm not ready for Davy Jones's locker yet. And as for you, Nina, stop fussing—I know what I'm doing!'

How could he? Nina brooded, when he didn't know the kind of man he was dealing with—a man who would do anything to get his own way. She should tell him, warn him, whatever the embarrassing consequences to herself.

'Any man with a bit of muscle can do basic carpentry,' Ray continued, obviously nettled at her interference. Since his arthritis had worsened over the winter, he had become ever more protective of his salty male pride. 'It only needs one of us to know what we're doing. I'll supervise. All Ryan here has to do is to use his common sense—of which he seems to have plenty—and follow my instructions. I'm the expert of the outfit. He's just the brawn, working for his keep.'

Ryan Flint—a brawny labourer working for his keep? Taking his orders from an irascible old codger who had nothing else to do but drive him crazy with his 'expert' supervision? Nina was startled by a new perspective on the situation, a bubble of malicious laughter rising hysterically in her throat.

How priceless! Oh, what a delicious irony it would be— Mr Arrogant Multimillionaire reduced to the level of a medieval serf, serving his lord with his sweated labour. The man who had wanted Karl sent to prison for daring to fall in love with his sister, trapped in the prison of his own making and cheerfully volunteering to do his sentence in hard labour!

Why not let him get on with it?

The sinful thought quickly blossomed into wicked fruit. A feeling of power swept over her, smothering her weak stirrings of conscience.

He was worried that he was broke and in trouble—why should she disabuse him? Why should she make anything easy for him? She was under no obligation to tell him what she knew. If she did and he left, she would never get another chance to make him pay. As a form of revenge it couldn't have been more perfect if she had planned it herself. And empowered by her knowledge, she would be in total control.

Oh, he'd eventually remember and then there would be trouble, but he would never be able to prove anything, and it would be worth it for the sheer pleasure of seeing him toiling like a common slave for a few days. She hoped he found it a humbling experience.

She tossed her head and gave him a haughty look. 'And if you get your memory back before the job's finished, what then? You just swan off and leave Ray in the lurch?'

Ryan's mouth thinned at the deliberate goad. 'Whatever happens, I'll finish what I start,' he said with a steely determination that satisfied her he was well and truly set up.

'Well, I suppose if you're going to be hanging around, you may as well make yourself useful,' she conceded grudgingly, turning away to hide her smirk. 'I'll leave you two to get on with it. You won't want to waste any time.'

She had to wipe the secret smile off her face a few seconds later, when Ryan joined her walking across the grass, leaving Zorro to the promise of the scrapings from the bacon pan.

'I need to change into something a bit more hard-wearing and practical if I'm going to be clambering over roofs,' he explained as Nina cast him a suspicious glance.

'You haven't *got* anything more hard-wearing,' she pointed out, having seen his washing drying by the fire.

'I know. I thought…well, I know Karl's clothes fit me, and you say he has plenty of others….'

He trailed off and Nina gave him a careless shrug of acquiescence. Poetic justice indeed. Talk about walking a mile in someone else's shoes!

'You changed your mind all of a sudden back there,' he said as they stepped over the low, straggly hedge between the two properties. 'One moment you're all fired up for me to leave and the next you're challenging me to stay.'

Ah...now they were getting to the *real* reason why he had been so quick to follow her.

'A woman's prerogative,' she murmured, tilting her face to enjoy the stroke of the sun on her skin and inhale the sharp tang of salt on the biting air.

His eyes followed the unconsciously sensual movement. 'You suddenly decided that I wasn't going to be a danger to myself and others?' he speculated. 'You decided I was worthy of your trust after all?'

'Not *you*...' She reacted crushingly to the hint of masculine satisfaction in his tone. '...*Ray*. I trust *his* opinion. I simply decided to give *you* the benefit of the doubt.' She turned her head, her green eyes cutting up at him. 'That's what every person deserves, don't you think...the chance to prove themselves?'

They had come to a halt by the open sliding door and Ryan rubbed his knuckles thoughtfully along his lower cheek—the same cheek, she was uneasily aware, that she had slapped on the night he had made the insulting suggestion that they work out their mutual differences in bed.

'Are you saying *that's* why you suddenly needed me to stay?' he asked quietly. 'You want me here purely as a matter of *principle?*'

Talk of principles, and the thread of disbelief in his voice made her flare defensively. 'I don't *need* you—I never even said I *wanted* you to stay! I'm willing to put up with you if I have to, that's all!'

His eyes were as hazy as a sea mist, moving in, enveloping her, reducing her visibility to a bare few centimetres.

'Oh, I think there's more to it than that, Nina.' He transferred his knuckles to her own satiny cheek, measuring the heat streaking beneath the skin. 'Much, much more...'

The trailing tip of his thumb brushed the corner of her mouth, which parted in alarm.

'Don't!' Her startled breath stirred the fine hairs on the back of his hand.

'Don't what?'

When had he moved so close? Why wasn't she pushing him away? What was it that rooted her to the spot and left her with only flimsy words with which to defend herself. *She* was supposed to be the one in control!

'Don't touch me!'

'Why not?' His voice dropped to a bittersweet tenderness, a mere scrape along her nerves. 'What are you so afraid of? What will happen if I do?'

She blinked in terror, breaking the hypnotic spell. 'Nothing!' She stiffened her sagging spine. 'Nothing will happen!'

Because she wouldn't let it!

'All right.' To her ineffable relief, his hand dropped away. 'I won't—' he turned into the house '—for now.' He gave her a smouldering smile over his shoulder. 'But we both know that I don't have to *touch* you for you to be *touched* by me, don't we…Nina, darling?'

And he strolled into the house, whistling…for all the world as if *he* were the one relishing revenge!

CHAPTER SIX

'I THINK you missed one!' Nina called out, lazily pointing up to the spot where a sun-blistered piece of weatherboard had sprung out from behind the trim at the top corner of the house.

Ryan, who had just set one foot on the grass after backing all the way down the tall extension ladder carrying his box of nails and a chisel and hammer, looked up, then down over his shoulder at Nina, standing next to Ray on his sandy front lawn, a folding canvas beach chair tucked under her arm, a plate of biscuits in her hand.

'Couldn't you have told me that while I was still up there?' he grunted.

'I didn't see it until just now,' Nina said innocently.

She watched him toil back up to the roof line, the faded denim of his dusty jeans straining at the seams as he braced rigid knees against the wooden rails of the ladder and hammered the board back into place. It was a sunny afternoon and he had taken off his shirt, his long, rangy back gleaming with a light coating of sweat, the lean muscles rippling as he worked.

'The boy makes a pretty picture, doesn't he?' Ray commented, shifting the splinter of wood he had been chewing to the side of his mouth. 'Thinking of painting him?'

Nina whipped her head around, scowling when she saw his lively expression. She handed him the biscuits she had baked for his afternoon tea. 'He's not a boy, and you know I don't do portraits.'

'I thought you might be making an exception in his

case...seeing as how much you seem to like watching him work,' he said slyly.

'He's so out of place he's rather difficult to ignore,' Nina defended herself.

'I thought he was fitting in quite well. He's certainly not a whiner. Does everything I ask and more. Got a good eye for detail. Doesn't even seem to get his back up when you come over to carp and criticise.'

'He doesn't belong here. I don't understand why you think he's so great,' she countered. She didn't like the fact that Ray and Ryan had established such a good rapport in such a short time. In little more than two days they seemed to have become as thick as thieves. It undermined her satisfaction in her petty revenge, which she had already discovered was rebounding on her in other unpleasant ways.

'It's a guy thing.' Nina's eyebrows whipped up incredulously and the old man chuckled. 'I picked that up from my granddaughter.' His faded grey eyes sobered. 'But, then, why shouldn't I like him, Nina? I've listened to him talk and my instincts tell me he's a good lad. What have you really got against him?'

She transferred her hold on the chair, hugging it to her chest like a shield. 'What's he been saying to you?' she demanded sharply.

'Probably nothing he wouldn't say to you...if you were interested enough to ask the right questions.'

Alarm flashed in Nina's eyes and her mouth pulled into a stubborn line. 'I just don't trust him, that's all.'

Ray chewed thoughtfully on his makeshift toothpick as he turned to watch Ryan start down the ladder again.

'Maybe it's not him you don't trust,' he said. 'Maybe your prejudices don't quite jell with what your own instincts are telling you. I wonder why you're so anxious to dislike him?'

And with a tug on the battered canvas hat covered with

fishhooks that he wore summer and winter, he stumped back over the grass, pausing for a word with Ryan before climbing the warped steps that were the next thing on his amateur workman's agenda and settling into his rocking chair on the porch, the plate of biscuits on his lap. Zorro, with his unerring instinct for a free feed, immediately rose from his lazy sprawl at the base of the ladder and skittered up to investigate the oaty aroma.

Ryan scooped up a plastic bottle of water from the ground and strolled across the grass to Nina, wiping his shiny forehead with the back of his arm, revealing the black tuft of hair in his damp armpit.

'What do you think?' he said, flicking his head towards the house.

Impressive, was Nina's impulsive response, but she kept her mouth sealed and quickly shifted her eyes from his chest to his workmanship. 'I still think you're a hairdresser.'

He grinned appreciatively at the put-down and crammed a biscuit into his mouth.

'Those weren't supposed to be for you,' she complained.

'Then why did you bake so many?'

'Anzac biscuits are Ray's favourite,' she said evasively.

'Mine now, too.' He took another one from his pocket and crunched into it with relish. 'I think Ray gets the better end of the deal he has with you—you're a good cook.'

She refused to be warmed by the praise. 'I like baking. I find it soothing.'

'Did you feel in need of a double batch of soothing this morning?'

He couldn't have known about her restless night...the haunted images of him that had pursued her even into sleep. She had spent far too much time over the past few days watching him, thinking about him, hugging her secret knowledge to herself and subtly tormenting him with his ignorance. That had meant seeking out his company instead of avoiding it, and too late she was realising that in doing so she was opening *herself* up to examination.

Her thoughts and feelings and past experiences were just as frequently the subject of the conversation as his, and since she was ostensibly eager to help him regain his memory, she could hardly object when he peppered her with questions about *her* amnesia in an effort to understand his own.

'I told you, I always bake extra Anzacs!' Fortunately, her words had the ring of truth.

A wink of light caught her eye—a bead of sweat rolling down his muscled shoulder. She stared at it in unwilling fascination as it hovered on the outer ridge of his collarbone.

'It's surprisingly hot work up there,' he said, following her gaze. He lifted the crumpled tail of the long-sleeved shirt he had tucked through his belt loop and slowly blotted at his upper chest and throat. 'I bet it gets scorching here in the summer. That metal roof traps a lot of heat, even in winter. I nearly fried like an egg scrambling around on it. I managed to peg everything back down, though, so Ray shouldn't have any leaks.'

It struck her that he was looking far too exhilarated for a slave-labourer. 'You're enjoying this!' she said accusingly.

He lowered the shirt from his face, his eyes blue with reflected sky. 'So are you,' he accused softly back. 'Or you were. Does it spoil your fun to find that I don't mind a bit of good, honest sweat? I wonder what it is you think you're trying to punish me for?'

'I had nothing to do with this. It was all *your* idea,' she reminded him hotly, all the while conscious of his credit-card holder burning a hole in her jeans pocket. 'I'm just an innocent bystander.'

His eyes responded with a brief blaze of white heat. 'Innocent? I don't think so. You're not a bystander, either. You're in this up to your sweet little neck whether you realise it or not.'

His cryptic words made her stiffen, and his hostility vanished as if he had flicked an internal switch.

'Where are you off to anyway?' He nodded at the chair, bulging with items that had been stuffed into the built-in pocket on the canvas back.

She was so grateful for the change of subject she answered frankly. 'Just down to the end of the beach. I want to do some sketches of the rocks.'

'Let me carry that for you.' Before she could refuse, he had plucked it out of her hands.

'I wasn't asking for company.'

She had couched her refusal too politely. 'I'm not company,' he said easily, heading towards the puriri trees that lined the bank. 'I'm the hired help.'

'And you already have a job to do,' she pointed out, hurrying after him to try to snag a chair leg.

'Ray told me to take a break.' He twisted his head to wave at the old man up on the porch, who flapped a gnarled hand in response. 'I think he was trying to figure out how to take a nap without missing anything. He certainly likes to be in charge!'

Nina was distracted from trying to wrest her property from his grasp. 'He's used to giving orders. He skippered a fishing boat until he was in his late sixties. He's not joking when he says he was married to the sea. I don't think he would've retired yet if it wasn't for his arthritis.'

'I wasn't criticising,' Ryan said, leaping lithely onto the sand and turning to extend a hand to help Nina down the grassy bank. 'I like the old guy. He's a battler. I hope I'm as feisty when I'm seventy-five.'

'He likes you, too.' Nina ignored his polite gesture and

was irritated to hear him chuckle as she ensured her jump onto the sand was just a little farther out than his.

'And that burns you up, doesn't it?' he guessed. 'I can't help it if I'm such a nice guy—'

'*Nice?*'

'You think that's too strong a word?'

No, too weak. Whatever words she was tempted to use to describe Ryan Flint, they weren't pallid, wishy-washy ones like 'nice'.

Nina shook the sand off the top of her sneakers and started to march briskly down the beach.

'Actually, I think he's just pleased to have a fresh audience for his tall tales,' Ryan said as he caught up. 'He certainly seems to have had plenty of adventures on the high seas. I suppose you've heard the one about the giant squid?'

Nina groaned. 'Many times. When I was a kid, it gave me nightmares!'

'That's right, you used to spend summer holidays here as a child, didn't you? Ray said your grandfather once owned the house you're renting, but that your grandmother sold it after he died when you were—what?—about thirteen?'

Ray must have certainly been extremely forthcoming during their cosy 'guy thing' chats over a couple of beers on the porch each evening, Nina thought nervously.

'Fifteen. Gran was only on a widow's benefit and she said she'd rather have the money for Karl and me to have a good education.' Which had made Karl's later decision to drop out of university a rather bitter pill, although Joan Dowling had never given any sign that she regretted her sacrifice.

'Were your parents fostering Karl before they died? Is that how he came to live with you and your grandparents?'

'My father's not dead—he took off just before my sister

was born,' she informed him with crisp detachment. 'He and Mum weren't married, so I suppose he figured he was under no obligation to stick around. Mum and Laurie were killed a year later when a gas heater exploded in our kitchen, but either my father didn't read the papers or he was afraid he might be asked to live up to his paternal responsibilities because he never even showed up for the funeral.' After eighteen—no, twenty years—the memory had lost most of the power to hurt.

'You were actually there when your mother was killed?' Ryan said, a slight hitch in his long stride.

'It was my birthday. Mum was wrapping my present. I was in the next-door neighbours' garden playing on their seesaw,' Nina recited automatically, as if by rote, before switching back to her original theme. 'Not that my grandparents would have let my father take me away from them even if he had turned up. But I was only six, and Gran didn't want me growing up as an only child, so she and Gramps fostered Karl the following year. Gran figured that his being younger than me would mean that at least I could have the familiarity of my big-sister role back.'

'You obviously took it seriously. Ray said you were always taking the blame for Karl's high jinks when you were younger.'

'Karl came from an abusive family,' Nina protested. 'He's always needed a lot of love.'

'Don't we all,' Ryan murmured and then laughed as, with a soft plop, Zorro sailed off the bank and landed beside them on the dry sand, legs already churning. He ran ahead, barking furiously, then circled back, nose down, following a Byzantine trail of invisible scents. 'I thought gluttony had got the better of him back there.'

'He probably knows about the biscuits in your pocket,' Nina said wryly.

'I suppose it's okay for him to run around without a leash?'

'Are you kidding? This is Shearwater. We don't go for the kind of suffocating regulations that you city dwellers do. And besides, there's no policeman on the island sum- mer *or* winter, so your chances of being apprehended for some petty misdemeanour are slim to none.'

'In other words, you make up all the rules yourselves and then decide individually whether you want to obey them or not. Sounds like anarchy to me.'

'I suppose personal freedom would sound like anarchy to an autocrat,' she said, stopping by the first outcropping of rocks—huge, weathered grey boulders buried halfway in the rippling sand, ancient remnants of the original cliffs.

'You think I'm dictatorial?'

'I think you like to believe you're right about every- thing,' she said tartly. 'That can make a man very domi- neering. You can put the chair down here.'

'Yes, ma'am, whatever you say, ma'am,' he mocked with his obsequious haste to obey.

He unfolded the squat metal legs of the chair, the low- slung seat almost touching the sand as he wedged it firmly into place. He waited until she sat down before, to her dismay, sprawling out on the sand beside her.

'You don't have to stay,' she said, twisting to get her sketchbook and pencils out of the chair pocket.

'I know.' He uncapped his bottle of water and took a long swallow. She couldn't help noticing the breeze stirring the silky triangle of hair on his chest.

'You should put your shirt back on,' she said, balancing the unopened sketchbook on her denim-clad thighs.

He screwed the cap back on the bottle and leaned over to place it behind them in the shadow thrown by her chair. 'I'm not cold.' His skin still glowed from the effects of his healthy exertions.

'You could still catch a chill. Once you stop moving, your muscles cool down very rapidly, and by the time you *feel* cold, it could be too late. You don't want to pull a muscle while you're up that ladder.'

'Yes, Mummy,' he jeered.

'Don't call me that!' There was a sharp snap as the pencil in her hand broke.

They both looked down at the damage and Ryan was first to react. He jackknifed to face her and lifted the clenched fist bearing the broken stump, carrying it swiftly to his lips.

'I'm sorry, Nina.' His apology whispered across her white knuckles, creeping into her guarded heart. 'I'm sorry...I shouldn't have teased you like that.'

'I—it's only a pencil,' she stammered, bewildered as to why she should suddenly feel like wildly weeping. And over a stupid *pencil!* She shook her head. 'It must have had a flaw. I have plenty of others.'

'Here, let me.' He unwrapped her stiff fingers and carefully picked the broken pieces of wood and graphite from the deep impressions in her skin, rubbing out the smudges from the graphite with his thumb. 'There...' he said soothingly.

He kissed the long, unbroken crease of her lifeline, and for an instant time was suspended with his black head bowed before her, his thick lashes dark crescents against his cheeks, his breath cupped in the palm of her hand.

Still holding her hand, he felt in the canvas pocket for another pencil and rewrapped her fingers around it. 'And look...I'm putting my shirt back on so I don't catch cold.'

He wrenched the brushed-cotton checked shirt from his belt loop and pulled it roughly on but left it unbuttoned, hanging loose off his shoulders so that she was still confronted by a wide expanse of naked chest as he knelt before her.

'What's the matter?'

'Nothing.'

His chest was rising and falling as if he had been running, and there was tension twitching at the glossy skin. The hair that was thick at the centre of his chest flared out across his pectoral muscles, thinning to a satiny smoothness around the caramel-coloured nipples. They had been blunt and flat when he drew on his shirt, but as she continued to stare at them they began to subtly change their conformation.

He looked down at himself and then slowly back up to her flushed face with heavy-lidded intent. 'You can touch them if you want.'

The fresh pencil fell out of her fingers as her hands curled helplessly on top of her sketchbook, and she fought the urge to do as he softly invited, the strange emotional turmoil of a few moments translating into something entirely different. Shouldn't she be outraged by the offer?

'Why would I want to?'

'Curiosity.'

He picked up her quivering hands and drew them to his chest, brushing them in delicate circles over the hairy skin until her fingertips nudged his brown nipples, which stiffened visibly to her touch. He continued to tease them lightly back and forth until her trailing fingers began to move of their own volition, drawing on the taut flesh until they were both breathing fast and hard.

'Am I allowed to be curious, too?' he asked huskily, and her bones melted as his eyes moved down over the stretchy ribbed sweater to the sharp points that strained against the cream wool. Her breasts felt unbearably full and heavy in the lace cups of her bra and it was a relief when he reached out to touch them, slowly tracing the thrusting outline of her rigid nipples through the twin layers of fabric.

'Just like me...' he whispered approvingly, his fingers

inscribing tight spirals around the throbbing peaks. 'Soft, yet excitingly hard.' He pinched gently, rolling his thumb and forefinger, and as she cried out, his open mouth came down over hers, moistly absorbing her honeyed moans, drinking in the taste of her sensual surrender.

His tongue played languidly with hers as he continued to lightly fondle her breasts, softly palming them while he concentrated on titillating the excited nipples, stoking her pleasure while not allowing it to reach a flashpoint beyond which it could flare out of his control. She leaned into him, trembling, her nails digging into his chest, and with a surge of bitter triumph he knew he could tumble her down onto the sand and mount her right there and then and she wouldn't lift a finger to resist. With his blitzing attack he had proved that he could seduce her into doing anything with him, everything…except…

Except the one most important thing. There was one thing that could not be forced, or physically seduced, that had to come freely from the heart or be worthless. As Ryan fought to control his own recklessly surging desire, the rancorous brooding of a seventeenth-century poet-lover mocked his memory and sickened his triumph.

If of herself she will not love,
Nothing can make her:
The devil take her!

She had to come to him in the full knowledge of what it meant or the conquest would be a Pyrrhic victory.

When Nina's hands began sinking lower on his chest, sliding down the tense ridges of his abdomen towards the band of his jeans, Ryan sucked in a sharp breath and stayed them with a wrenching curse.

'Ryan…?'

'You came out here to sketch, remember?' he said, easing himself away from her mouth with a series of biting kisses. He relaxed back on the sand, drawing up his knees to ease the pressure of his jeans on his fierce erection.

The second pencil had rolled off her sketchbook and dropped by her feet, and Nina reached shakily down for it, her mouth and breasts still hotly throbbing, mortified by her wanton behaviour and the fact that Ryan, not she, had been the one to call a halt.

Suddenly, a small shower of cold water hit her, practically hissing as it landed on her burning cheeks.

'Zorro!' Her voice blended with Ryan's in a scolding chorus. The small dog finished shaking the sea water from his spiky coat and regarded them with a cocked head, tongue lolling from his open jaw.

'And the dish ran away with the spoon,' Ryan muttered, buttoning up his shirt

'What?' Nina asked as she shook off her sketchbook.

'The little dog laughed to see such sport,' he recited dryly.

It gave her a strange pang to hear his deep voice quoting nursery rhymes and she hurriedly transferred her attention to Zorro. It *did* look as if Zorro was grinning at them, she thought.

'You little wretch!' she threatened. 'If my book had been open and you'd got the pages wet, you would have been in real trouble.'

Ryan sifted about in the surrounding sand and unearthed a short piece of driftwood, which he hurled down onto the wet sand, sending Zorro hurtling in pursuit to snatch it from the encroaching waves.

'He was probably just tired of being ignored.'

Nina refused to blush. She folded over the loose leaves of her sketchbook until she reached a fresh page, which she dated along the bottom. 'He's used to amusing himself when he invites himself along on my sketching trips,' she countered.

Zorro returned with his lump of wood and had it thrown for him again.

'Then maybe he was jealous.'

She gritted her teeth and stared resolutely at the grouping of weed-covered rocks she had come to sketch.

'He's never been known to get bored with a game of fetch,' she felt bound to warn him.

'That's okay. I'm a patient man,' he said, which she didn't believe for a moment.

But so it proved, and as the game continued, Nina began to relax and find her creative impulses surprisingly unhindered by the unsettling company. Zorro's timely intervention had defused a fraught situation and his continuing antics further dissipated the tension until Nina was absently chatting as she sketched, describing in idyllic terms the childhood summers she had spent on Shearwater Island.

'Do you think that's why you were on the ferry that day, why you were coming here? You were pursuing those unsullied memories of golden summers, when life was safe and secure—all childish pleasures and no responsibilities?'

Nina's pencil hatched in a patch of shade around the base of the rock. 'I never really thought about it, but…yes, I suppose that could have been what drew me here and why I felt such a powerful urge to stay. Shearwater is magical, a perfect artist's retreat. It's also where I got my first set of real artists' watercolours—Ray gave them to me the Christmas I was nine.'

'He says you're so ensconced here that you never leave the island.'

'He exaggerates.' With a few expert flicks of a craft knife, Nina trimmed her pencil and went back to work. 'It's not as if I'm a recluse. I've been over to Waiheke a few times, to the library and to buy supplies. One of the craft shops over there sells my paintings on commission, and also my note cards—I do scenic watercolour sketches on handmade paper that a neighbour over the hill makes. The cards sell really well and they're quite fun to do because they're so small and I can be completely spontaneous.'

She held her breath, wondering if the talk of art might trigger a shaft of remembrance, but the moment slipped past as Ryan squinted at a boat sailing in around the point. While the patchy and wildly uneven return of his memories had become a source of escalating guilt and anxiety for Nina, he seemed to have adopted an attitude of resolute acceptance, a determination to treat the whole unpredictable episode as a holiday. Perhaps, subconsciously, he was aware that he *was* on holiday in his real life and his biorhythms had adjusted accordingly.

'Why do you think *you* came here?' She turned the question on him, intensely bothered by the coincidence. The islands of the gulf seemed an unsophisticated holiday destination for such a wealthy, worldly, cultivated man.

'Perhaps I was looking for something magical, too.'

'You don't strike me as the sort of man who believes in magic—except as a clever conjuring trick,' she countered, her voice unknowingly reflecting his cynical tone.

'There's a part of all of us that wants to believe in magic,' he said quietly. 'The innocent child in us...'

Nina turned abruptly away and the conversation languished. Ryan took Zorro down to where the hard-packed wet sand was pricked with air bubbles, to show him that digging for live crabs was much more exciting than chasing a boring old stick. Returning, he lay on his back and dozed, and Nina's pencil flew across the paper. A while later, when he stirred, she quickly turned the page and began to sketch Zorro, visible only as a pair of hind legs and perky tail protruding from the hole he was digging to China.

Ryan got up, dusting the sand from his jeans and stretching lazily. 'I guess I'd better go back to work,' he said, yawning. 'See you later. By the way, Ray said to tell you someone's given him a bundle of fresh scallops that we can have for dinner.'

He was practically drooling as he spoke, and she remembered the scallops in mornay sauce that he had ordered at the expensive restaurant to which Karl had invited what he hoped was his future bride and her brother to dine. But instead of being impressed by his generous hospitality, Ryan had provoked an argument that had ended with Karl and Katy storming out just as their main course arrived, leaving Nina to cope with an embarrassing situation and a smouldering fellow diner who had relished her discomfort and insisted on their finishing the meal.

Since he had magnanimously offered to pay the impending huge bill, for which Karl had failed to make arrangements as he had angrily swept out, Nina—with only a few dollars in her purse and no credit card—had been compelled to agree. She had been forced to spend another hour of verbal fencing that had left her feverish and flustered as Ryan's sophisticated teasing had skilfully inflamed her emotions, ripping away the calm facade with which she had been trying to handle him.

'Maybe you're allergic to shellfish,' she called after his retreating back, goaded by the memory of that sultry evening and the steamy goodnight kiss he had punished her with under the amused eyes of the restaurant doorman before handing her into the waiting taxi and tossing a fifty-dollar note through the window for what he knew was only a twenty-dollar fare. 'You'd better not have any!'

He glanced back over his shoulder, his eyes glinting with a challenge that made her insides shiver. 'As it happens, I've just remembered. I love all kinds of seafood.'

'How very convenient,' she muttered suspiciously as he strolled away, his hips rolling in a masculine swagger that was as arrogant as it was sexy, an impossibly well-behaved Zorro meekly coming to heel at a single command.

That brooding suspicion was still with her hours later as she packed up her sketchbook and retraced her steps, carefully avoiding looking up at Ray's house as she skulked along below the bank of puriri trees until she was parallel with her door, then scuttled across her lawn.

It was a suspicion that had been hovering in the back recesses of her mind, but one she had been loath to drag out into the light of day for fear of the consequences if it were true.

It nagged at her as she rattled about her studio, assembling the completed set of watercolours that George was due to collect the next day, then eventually drove her down to Ryan's room where her hand hovered sweatily on the doorknob.

What she was about to do was an unforgivable invasion of privacy, but she had a *right* to do this, she told herself. She had a right to protect herself.

His bag was still sitting under the bed and Nina was startled at its weight as she slid it out. She had thought Ryan would have preferred to put his clothes in the drawers or wardrobe rather than leave them zipped in his bag, and in any case, surely his clothes alone wouldn't be very heavy.

The first thing she saw when she pulled down the zip was a cell phone, not the slim accessory that Dave Freeman had carried, but the solid, seriously expensive, cutting-edge communications device that accepted faxes and e-mails and probably satellite communications, as well.

Nina picked it up. Perhaps he hadn't considered it worth mentioning because it had been rendered useless by the rain, she thought hopefully, removing it from its leather case, but when she pushed the power button, it sprang to life and she saw from the digital display that its long-life battery was fully charged.

It felt cool and heavy in her hand, but the shape and weight of it also felt queasily familiar. She had held this phone before...used it herself. She didn't need an instruction booklet to tell her how to work its complex commands.

A veil billowed in her memory and she quickly twitched it back into place, drawing out the credit-card holder from her pocket and punching in the toll-free number on the back of one of the credit cards.

'Hello, I'm calling on behalf of my—my boss who's lost his platinum card while on holiday. I'd like to make sure you cancel it, please,' she said croakily, reeling off Ryan's name and the string of numbers embossed on the holo-grammed silver surface.

She heard the sound of a computer being keyed and then the disembodied toll of doom. 'Mr Flint rang and person-ally cancelled that card himself two days ago. According to his instructions, we're withholding the issue of a new one until he gets back from his trip.'

'Oh, I see. Sorry, I must have misunderstood,' Nina managed to say before she hung up.

He had cancelled his missing credit cards two days ago.

With no more thoughts of discretion or hiding the evidence of her search, she ripped back into the bag, but the only other thing inside was a heavy rectangle wrapped like contraband inside the doubled-up black sweater he had worn when he arrived. What had he been so anxious to prevent from being casually discovered?

Snagging her fingernails on the fine wool in her hurry, Nina sat on the bed and impatiently wrenched the item free.

A hardback book?

He had been hiding an interest in *reading*?

A thin, grey-haired man in a tweed suit gazed up at her with an enigmatic smile from the water-stained back dust jacket. A bookmark sprouted from roughly the halfway point, and as she gingerly turned it over, she could see that edges of the pages were rippled where dampness had seeped into the body of the book.

The title took up the whole front cover.

Mind and Memory: Case Studies of Amnesia. A string of medical qualifications followed the author's name.

Ryan had been come to Shearwater Island carrying a book all about memory loss?

She was so stunned that the full implication didn't hit her until several heartbeats later.

Oh, *God*...!

'Have you seen enough? Or do you want to strip-search me, too?'

Nina's head jerked up and she stared blindly at the man standing grimly in the doorway. How long had he been watching her paw through his things?

She jumped to her feet clutching the book and grabbed the cell phone from the bed with some wild idea of confiscating everything that he could possibly use as a threat. He was obviously expecting some form of answer, but Nina was incapable of giving it to him. She headed towards the door, but instead of pausing for the confrontation he had invited, she shouldered past him with a sudden burst of superhuman strength that sent him staggering into the sharp edge of the wooden moulding.

'Nina, wait...'

Cursing, he raced after her down the hall, bursting into the living room and hurdling over the couch to bar her way to the sliding door with his outflung arms.

'Nina, don't think you're going to run away from th—'

'You bastard!' she screamed at him. She hadn't been running away; she had been seeking a space large enough to encompass her towering rage. She threw the phone directly at his head, all the strength of her shoulder behind her deadly accurate aim, but he ducked and it crashed against the frame of the window, sending a shiver through the toughened glass.

'For God's sake, Nina—that could have killed me!'

'I wish it had, you lying, slimy creep!' She followed it up with the heavy book, this time aiming for a bigger target, and it hit him square in the centre of his chest. A cough of pain wheezed out of his lungs as he doubled over, rubbing his heart. 'No wonder you had a "textbook" presentation of amnesia!'

'God, Nina—'

He could beg for mercy until hell froze over and she wouldn't listen. 'There's nothing wrong with your memory—there never has been. It was all a set-up! You were stringing me along. You knew *exactly* who you were all the time!'

'That's not entirely true,' he defended himself through another harsh cough. 'I was dazed at first. I wasn't sure what was real and what wasn't—'

'Don't *lie!*' she shrieked. 'I can prove it. I had the credit cards you supposedly didn't even know you owned—the cards you rang up and cancelled because you thought they were lost! Well, here they are back again. Take them—I never wanted them. They're as worthless as you are!' She tore them out of the holder and threw them at him one by one, followed by the stack of business cards that struck him on the cheek and scattered like confetti over the floor.

He rubbed his cheek, ice filming his eyes as he looked at the scattered cards at his feet. '*You* had these?' he grated harshly. 'You've had them all along?'

She would have liked to torment him by saying yes, but she wasn't going to give him an excuse to accuse her of trying to steal them. 'No, I found them down the back of the couch the morning Ray got home, and when I looked at them…I phoned your office and then I *knew*…I *remembered.*'

He went white.

'You've got your memory back,' he said, his voice boiling with black bitterness. 'You bitch! You knew *two days ago* and you didn't *tell* me? Who's been stringing who along…*babe?*'

His insolent sneer fueled her blazing temper. 'Why should I have told you? I don't owe you anything. And, unlike you, my amnesia is not a sick joke I play on people for my own sadistic ends. I haven't got my memory back, only the small chunk of it that confirms what a twenty-four-carat-gold bastard you are.'

Ryan snapped to rigid attention, his eyes narrowing to splinters of blue ice as she continued to blaze away at him with bullets of contempt.

'What I *remember* is a couple of months I rather *would* forget, a couple of months of you making my brother's life a misery—' Her breath caught on a humiliating sob.

'That's *it?*' He snapped out the hoarse question as he started prowling towards her. 'That's all…a couple of *months* nearly three years ago? You don't remember any more than that?'

Her fists bunched helplessly at her sides. 'That's all I *need* to remember as far as you're concerned—'

'Oh, no, it isn't,' he cut her off savagely, moving in closer, his eyes locked on her furious face. 'Oh, no…I haven't finally tracked you down to be fobbed off like that.'

Tracked her down?

'I don't know what you're talking about.'

His voice was low, purposefully intent. 'I'm talking about you and me, babe.'

Her breath dug a hollow in her chest. 'There is no "you and me",' she denied in a thin, high voice.

'How do you know?' he said cruelly. 'You're hiding out

here on your magical little island, hiding from all the things you don't want to remember, things that *I* don't have any choice but to live with.'

Nina felt a tremor of deep foreboding. 'It's not that I don't *want* to, it's that I *can't*—'

'Not yet. But you will by the time I've finished with you,' he said brutally. 'I'm not leaving until I get what I want.'

'And what's that, for God's sake?' she cried wildly.

His expression was dark and saturnine, his smile a caricature of tenderness. 'How about the two years you and I spent together? How about the money you stole when you walked out on me without so much as a goodbye kiss?'

'What *money*? Are you insane?' A sick thrill whipped through her veins. 'Two *years*? Are you suggesting that you and I—that I—that we were... That you and I had some sort of *affair*?' she choked, putting a hand up to her swirling head.

'You lived in my house and slept in my bed. It was more than just an *affair*.'

'No, I don't believe you...' As the velvety blackness closed comfortingly in, she felt his strong arms closing around her gracefully collapsing body.

'Swoon all you like, my faithless darling. I'll still be here when you wake up. This time, there's going to be no easy escape....'

CHAPTER SEVEN

NINA opened the door of her flat, her body tightening at the sight of Ryan Flint on the doorstep, looking wildly out of place in the shabby hall in his silk suit and cashmere coat. She hadn't seen him since the fight outside the courthouse the previous week. She had thought she might never see him again.

'You shouldn't have come here...' Her husky voice faltered at the smouldering impatience in the pale blue eyes.

'May I come in?'

She fell back and he stepped over the threshold, slanting himself sideways as he moved past her in the confined space of the narrow entranceway, his long coat brushing against the neat blouse and slender navy skirt she had worn to work.

'If this is about Karl—'

He stopped her with a single look, shouldering out of his coat and throwing it over the back of a chair. The tiny flat, which had seemed so achingly empty and depressingly sad since Gran had died, was suddenly throbbing with vibrant, restless life. Except for Karl, she had never had a man here. Looking after Gran had been emotionally draining as well as physically taking up all her spare time and energy.

He didn't even look around the tiny flat as he took off his jacket and loosened his silk tie, his eyes moving over her flushed face and primly attired figure, lingering on the crisply concealing blouse and the lush curve of her hips encased in the tight skirt that ended halfway up her thighs. His nostrils flared as he eased his collar open and saw her

115

gaze follow the movement, her lips parting at the glimpse of the bronzed hollow of his throat.

'Do you have anything to drink?'

His blunt demand cloaked the crackling sexual tension with a thin veneer of sociability. Nina's fingers tracked the side seams of her skirt, smoothing it over her hips in an unconsciously seductive gesture.

'I—I might have some Scotch...' She knew she did. Towards the end, the smooth liquor was the one small pleasure that Gran had still been able to enjoy, with the added bonus that it helped dull the pain the drugs no longer seemed to ease.

Ryan followed her into the cramped galley kitchen while she fumbled the glasses out of the cupboard, moving up to catch the whisky bottle when it threatened to slip through her trembling hands, then taking over the pouring of two stiff drinks.

'I—I'm sorry, I'm not sure I've got anything to mix with it,' she said vaguely, finding it difficult to think while he was so close, his lean body angled towards hers, crowding her with intense awareness of his masculinity, the musky scent of him even more potent than the heady aroma of the Scotch.

'That's all right, I'm not thirsty anyway,' he said roughly, shoving the glasses away and spinning her into his arms.

His mouth crashed heavily down on hers, smothering her whimper of relief as the momentum of his body crushed her back against the kitchen wall. Nina's head angled beneath his as she frantically tried to deepen his savage kisses, her hands tearing at the buttons of his pale grey shirt, pulling it open so that she could lace her fingers through the hair on his chest.

She felt him shudder as she scraped her nails across his skin, his strong hands sliding up the outside of her thighs, working her skirt up around her waist, pushing her panty hose and fragile lace panties out of the way so that he could reach her molten core. His fingers slid against her slippery heat, his knees pushing in between hers to wedge her legs farther apart while he prepared her for his urgent posses- sion—'

'*No!*'

Nina's eyes flew open, her panting cry dying on her lips as she found herself lying on the couch in the house at Puriri Bay, staring up into Ryan's waiting gaze. The press of his hip as he sat alongside her was all too familiar.

'No...' she protested weakly, caught between two equally unacceptable realities.

'Yes...I'm still here,' he confirmed remorselessly. 'I told you I wasn't going anywhere. I'm part of your magical world now.' He stroked her hair back from her hot forehead in a gesture of mingled triumph and reassurance. 'You were only out for a few seconds.'

A few seconds! Nina shuddered. Her mind was playing tricks on her. She didn't know what to believe any more. Only she knew—in her heart she knew—that that frenzied coupling against the wall of her flat had been no erotic fantasy. No fantasy she had invented had ever been that vividly explicit!

'You said you tracked me down,' she said in a feathery whisper. 'Why? How?'

His hand returned to the back of the couch, bracing his leaning body across her.

'Since you haven't entered any database or made any official applications or opened any bank or utility accounts since you got here, it wasn't easy. It was pure chance. The daughter of a friend bought a watercolour of yours on a trip to Waiheke. Your style might have matured almost out of recognition, but your signature is still that distinctive *N*. So I made a few discreet inquiries about the artist—'

'What do you know about my style?' she broke in jerkily, thinking of that intimidating gallery where paintings sold for thousands of dollars rather than the mere couple of hundred that she commanded for some of her larger works.

'I had a studio built for you at my house.' His mouth twisted. 'It was one of the major inducements for you to come and live with me—that you could spend your free hours in the studio, painting.'

The wall in her mind shivered on its rock-solid foundations. 'You're lying,' she said, desperately grasping at straws. 'Even if we had been lovers, I wouldn't have moved in with you—I couldn't have done that to Karl.'

'Neither of us had a lot of choice in the matter,' he said wryly. 'Our body chemistry was too strong. We were like two halves of a biological equation. Karl had nothing to do with what happened between us.'

'How can you say that? He was the reason we met. You were the one who got him arrested—'

'He got *himself* arrested,' Ryan corrected harshly. 'Karl was in trouble before I ever came along, and you know it. He would have dragged Katy down with him, too. He got in too deep with the wrong people and ended up having to pay the price for it. He was damned lucky he didn't have to do any jail time.'

Nina felt a tremor of relief as he looked grimly down on her.

'Karl might have preferred to blame me, and yes, it suited me to let him think I had that kind of muscle, but I make it a point never to involve the police in my personal conflicts. I much prefer to deal with my enemies in my own time on my own terms.' His faintly cruel smile sealed the sincerity of his words.

Nina shivered. Was she his enemy now?

'If it were true...about you and me, Karl would have

told me...' Her voice petered out as she pressed her hands against her face. 'He *did* tell me. I *couldn't* have been living with you. He told me that after Gran died, I travelled around...backpacking, never staying in one place long enough to settle down.'

'He lied. You never went anywhere. You were with me.' Ryan's implacable certainty hammered the words into her skull. 'Karl still hates my guts for seeing through his charming facade, for opening up Katy's eyes to his real character, and yes, for opening yours, too. When we became lovers, it was obvious you were choosing me over him, and that ate at him. We were happy and he only had himself to blame for his misfortune—that was reason enough for the selfish bastard to resent our relationship.

'He was one of the first people I got in touch with when you disappeared.' He drove his point home with painful precision. 'He visited you on the day you left and claimed you were talking about taking off to Australia to ''find yourself''. He told me to leave you alone, that you didn't need me any more. He's known all this time what happened to you, where you were, that you'd lost your memory— and yet he never bothered to tell either one of us about the other. Ask yourself why that is, Nina, *why*.'

'Why should I believe anything you say?' Nina swung her legs off the couch and stood up. 'You know I can't remember. For all I know, you could be making all this up.'

His hand on her arm steadied her swaying body, turning her to face him. 'Why don't you call Karl, then?' he challenged. 'Tell him that I'm here on the island and see what happens.'

Her upturned face paled, her green eyes glowing at him with bewildered mistrust. His rigid face softened, his hand relaxing on her arm, stroking down to cup her elbow and coaxing her gently forward until their bodies were almost touching.

'Or, better still, why don't you come back home with me now and find out for yourself?' he murmured. 'See if being back in familiar surroundings makes a difference to what you can remember. That book you threw at me—you should read it, Nina. It can help you understand what's happening to you. It says that physical cues can be a powerful source of spontaneous recall. Cues from your senses— familiar sights, sounds, tastes, sensations...'

Like the sensational impact of his lovemaking! Nina began to shake her head, but he continued inexorably.

'Seeing your studio, your clothes, your personal things, how we lived...that could help make it real to you.'

'No, I'm not going anywhere with you!' she said, her thoughts in a hopeless tangle of panic. 'If it's true and I left you...I—I ran away, I must have had a good reason—'

'Why don't you come back with me and together we can discover what that is?'

His voice was soft, sombre, infinitely seductive. It promised safety, yet Nina sensed an unspeakable danger in his deliberate gentling.

'If we were so happy, why would I have left?' she demanded shrilly. 'Was it another woman? Did I catch you sleeping with someone else?'

His gentleness dropped away into the well of his frustration. 'Aren't you going to ask if I was beating you, too?'

She realised it had never even occurred to her as a possibility. He was undoubtedly tough, even ruthless in the pursuit of his goals, but on some instinctive level she didn't believe he was abusive. Only too sexy for his own good...

'You're avoiding the question,' she snapped, relieved to be able to turn the tables, albeit only briefly.

'I was faithful to you every minute we were together—

just as I've been uncomfortably celibate for the past nine months,' he snapped back.

Her cheeks stung. 'Celibate?' Somehow she had difficulty associating Ryan Flint with the word.

His eyes gleamed wolfishly. 'Can't you tell? I'm aching for a woman, Nina. The only drawback is the woman I'm aching for is trying to pretend she doesn't want to know me.'

She took a deep, shaky breath and walked away to pick up the fallen book and thrust it out at him. 'I want you to leave.'

He seemed genuinely sympathetic. 'I know you do. But I can't, Nina. I never walk out on unfinished business.'

She threw the book down on the couch. 'If you're talking about this money you're claiming I took—'

He named a sum of cold, hard cash that took her breath away. 'It disappeared from the safe in our bedroom the same day you did your daylight flit, and since you were the only other person to have the combination—'

'Why do you assume it wasn't simply a burglary?' she flung at him.

'A burglar would have cleared out the safe. There were a lot of other valuable things in there, but all that went missing was the cash and your passport and personal papers.'

She realised that he had trapped her into arguing as if she believed his tale about their being live-in companions.

'I didn't have any of those things when I arrived here. You *are* delusional.' She paced the room, waving her hands. 'Look around you. Does it *look* as if I'm rolling in stolen money? What I have, I *earned*.' And she was fiercely proud of the way she had done it!

He shrugged. 'Maybe you went straight to the casino and gambled it all away. You might have thought that was rough justice, considering the way I originally made my money.'

'I don't gamble.'

'The whole of life is a gamble.'

She didn't like the idea of being at the mercy of the random rules of chance. 'What did the police say when you reported it? Are they looking for me, too?'

'I told you, I don't like the police poking into my private affairs. You could call it a legacy from my childhood.'

'Your childhood?' She found herself teetering on the brink of understanding.

'My parents are a very charming pair of con artists,' he admitted, nudging her over the edge. *She already knew this,* she thought as she listened to him. 'They dragged Katy and me all over the world in pursuit of their grand scams, even using us to help reel in the suckers when we got old enough to tell a convincing lie. I struck out on my own as soon as I could, but that left Katy to their tender mercies.

'When they finally settled in Australia after a big score, she and I thought she would have her chance at a decent education and a stable life, but Max and Irene found respectability boring. So they pulled up stakes and went back to their swindles, but this time Katy was old enough to kick up a fuss and I was able to persuade them to leave her with me.'

I have a duty to stand between my sister and harm, she remembered him telling her in the exhausted aftermath of the encounter in the kitchen of her flat. *I haven't always been there for her when she needed me. I owe it to her to be there for her now. I always protect my own.*

His expression became sardonic. 'One thing my parents taught me that I *did* consider good advice—make sure you always have a cash float stashed away for emergencies, preferably in untraceable, small used bills.'

'So you have no record of ever having had the money

and never told the police it was missing,' Nina guessed shrewdly. 'In other words, you have no proof of anything you say!'

'I have all the proof I need in here.' He pointed to his temple.

'So you're out for revenge. Is that what all this is about?' Nina demanded, hands on hips. In a twisted kind of way, it would be a relief!

The man wanted his money back. He would soon have to accept that she didn't have it. She had never been materialistic. Clothes, jewellery, possessions—they had never been more important to her than people.

'Not revenge. Satisfaction.'

'What's the difference?' she challenged unwisely.

He smiled. 'Come here and I'll show you,' he purred.

She bridled at the sudden change in his demeanour. 'If I walked out on you, how can you still want anything to do with me? Have you no pride?' she ripped at him.

'Oh, you've already stripped me of that, Nina, so what do I have to lose? But if you assume I'm going to grovel to get you back in my bed, you have another think coming. You're the one who'll be doing the begging.'

Her eyes blazed with a fury that made him laugh, enraging her even more. 'The hell I am! What's the matter, can't your ego accept that you're obviously completely forgettable in bed?'

'Liar,' he goaded. 'I slept with you for two years. I know your body as well as you do. I know all the nuances of its language. You can close your mind to our relationship, but your body definitely remembers how good we were together. You're as hot for me right now as I am for you. Arguments always did spice up our sex life.'

She spluttered, her hand itching to slap his face as she had once before. 'Get out!'

'No way. I'm bonding to you like superglue from now

on, sweetheart. The only way you'll get rid of me is to stick a knife in my chest.'

She went white, then red. 'Don't tempt me!' she choked.

'Oh, I intend to tempt you every which way,' he said, then turned towards the kitchen. 'Starting with your taste-buds.'

Another lightning switch of moods to set her off balance.

'What are you doing?' she asked, following him suspiciously, still spoiling for a fight.

'Making dinner,' he said, rattling through the cupboards and getting out a shallow pan and three beautiful, oval pottery ramekins from the set of crockery Nina had got for giving painting lessons to the potter's ten-year-old daughter. 'Ray gave me the scallops and a bottle of white wine he brought back from his daughter's.'

He fetched them from the fridge, where he must have detoured before continuing along to his room to catch her red-handed in her search, and began assembling his other ingredients. He drew a broad chef's knife out of the knife block on the bench and extended it to her, handle first.

'Care to do some chopping?' His eyes were gleaming as brightly as the wicked, shiny blade. He wasn't kidding about temptation!

She was baffled by his good humour. 'I don't want you in my kitchen,' she said truculently. That he liked to cook was already evident from the amount of time he had spent there during his visit. If he had got his way, he would have cooked for them every night.

He found her sullenness amusing. 'You'd rather have me in your bedroom, I know, but I did tell you that you'd have to beg me first.' He swung around to the bench and began to rinse the scallops, expertly separating the coral from the beard.

'I usually just crumb and fry them when they're this fresh,' she criticised.

'Then it will be a special treat for you to have them done differently for a change,' he said, deftly cutting a lemon and squeezing out the juice. 'We all have to adapt to changes in our lives, Nina. As difficult as it may be to accept sometimes, change is good. Birth, life and death is a natural progression—'

'I thought you were supposed to be cooking, not offering a lesson in pop psychology,' she said sharply.

'I can do both,' he said modestly. 'And since you seem to have avoided anyone with the medical expertise to help you assess your amnesia, I've elected myself the self-educated expert. Ray said you've never even consulted an M.D.'

'I didn't need to. I was fit and healthy and perfectly normal in every other way—'

'You mean you didn't want anyone to deny you your regression to childhood.'

'How can I have matured as an artist if I've been regressing to childhood?' she snapped.

The smooth rhythm of the knife paused. 'Because you put all your passion into your paintings and none into your life.'

'That's not true!'

He shook the knife at her. 'Be honest. You feel more emotionally stirred up at this moment, more alive, yelling at me, than you've felt since you arrived here.'

'I am not yelling!'

'Zorro thinks you are.'

Nina looked at the dog lying guard in front of the fridge, his nose on the cold floor, his ears folded closed.

Traitor!

'What are you making anyway?' she asked with exaggerated softness.

'*Coquilles Saint-Jacques*—'

'That's just a fancy name for scallops,' she scoffed.

'—à la Flint. My variation provides an exquisite touch of something unique in the sauce.' He tipped her a sly, sexy wink. 'You'll recall I'm very good at exquisite variations, Nina. I have great endurance and I always like to be inventive.'

She glowered at him, folding her arms over her tautening breasts. 'Really? Well, I have better things to do than stand around watching you play chef.'

As an exit line, it was a dismayingly limp white flag, and she fled to her studio to simmer and stew over the coruscating riposte she *should* have uttered.

In order to take her mind off the emotional turmoil generated by the stunning revelations from her past, she buried herself in the pleasantly mindless task of stretching the paper that she would be using the next day, and when she finally heard a deep voice calling, she reluctantly emerged to find a mouth-watering aroma permeating the kitchen and Ryan removing the bubbling ramekins from under the oven grill and setting them on the hob.

He had showered and changed out of his work clothes into his black trousers and white linen shirt, and Nina immediately wished she had done a bit more than merely wash her hands and brush her hair and swap her ribbed sweater for a loose blouse.

'I've set the table, but if you wouldn't mind pouring the rest of the wine, I'll just carry this one over to Ray—'

Nina snatched up an oven mitt and tea-towel and reached for the third ramekin before he could pick it up. 'I'll take it!'

'If you're thinking of running to Ray with a sob-story of what a brute I am, hoping that he'll kick me out and tell me never to darken his door again, forget it. He already knows our history together. I told him who I was the first time we met.'

Fortunately, Nina hadn't picked up the scalding dish. 'What do you mean, you told him who you were?'

He shrugged. 'Basically, I told him that I didn't have amnesia, that I was here in order to get the love of my life back. *He* was the one who came up with the idea of having me work on his house, to give me an excuse to hang around you.'

'You *devil!*' As a pre-emptive strike, it was masterful. Ray, for all his pride in his crusty bachelor status, was a romantic at heart.

The love of his life. How beautifully lyrical Ryan made it sound, but in all his earlier talk of passion and desire and body chemistry and biological equations, he had never even hinted that his heart was involved. He had never tried to flatter her into believing that he had been *in love* with her. Why? Because he obviously knew it wouldn't have been convincing. He might persuade an old man who had never met him before that he was an old-fashioned, swashbuckling romantic hero, but Nina was made of sterner stuff.

He grinned. 'It always pays to stack the odds. I think you'll find Ray's on my side in this one.'

When she marched across to deliver the steaming dish, she discovered he was right.

Ray looked at her from under lowered bushy eyebrows when she stiffly expressed her hurt for his part in the deception.

'It's past time,' he said gruffly. 'Ryan's right—you can't keep hiding things from yourself, pretending that a part of you doesn't exist. The past has come right back to meet you, girl. You have to deal with it before you can properly get on with the rest of your life. And if this lad is the one to help you do that, well, good on him.'

Nina couldn't find it in her heart to be really angry with the old man when it was clear that he was stubbornly convinced that he had her best interests at heart.

'You certainly did a good snow job on him,' Nina began when she slammed back into the house a few minutes later. 'What're you going to do with that?'

Ryan was spooning a portion of scallops and a smothering of sauce onto a plastic plate. 'It's for Zorro.'

'You can't give him all that,' she protested as he set it down on the floor. 'It's got wine and cheese in it. It'll be far too rich for his stomach!'

They both watched as the scallops disappeared in a twinkling of an eye, following by a noisy sucking of sauce and a credible attempt to eat the plate.

'You can be the one to get up in the night when he's whimpering with a stomach-ache,' she said sourly.

There was a split second of silence, a mutual holding of breath, then life moved on again, and Nina decided she had imagined the splinter of pain that had entered her heart before the echo of her words died away.

Much as she would have liked to turn her nose up at Ryan's meal, it turned out to be delicious, and the glass of wine she had fully intended to spurn was the perfect accompaniment. She limited herself to one confidence-inspiriting glass, however, since she badly needed to keep her head.

With darkness pressing in on the windows around them, the low, pendant light centred over the table and the glowing fire in the grate were the only illuminations, creating a bubble of intimacy that made Nina vibrantly aware of the man across the table, acutely conscious of the spell he was weaving as he set out to be a relaxed and entertaining companion, talking art until she warmed to the lively discussion and making her laugh when she should have been guarded and wary.

He watched her greedily eat every bite of his meal with no sign of gloating. 'Actually, I thought I might become a chef once,' he confided, pouring himself the rest of the wine. 'As a teenager, I worked in the kitchen of a hotel-casino. Only that's when I discovered I had more of a flair for the front of the house than the rear,' he said wryly. 'I learnt to deal cards and never looked back.'

'Easy money?' she gibed.

He considered the question seriously. 'No, I wouldn't say it was easy. It takes intense concentration, skill, practice, persistence and, of course, a certain amount of luck to beat the house odds. I always knew that it wasn't something I wanted to do for the rest of my life. I was looking for a stake I could use to enter the next phase of my life. It was serendipity that the stake turned out to *be* the next phase. Among the dubious benefits of being the son of a con man was that I was exposed to lots of fine art in public and private collections while we were racketing around Europe pretending to be rich.'

'And now you don't have to pretend any more. You're a rich and influential art collector yourself.'

He looked at her across the top of his glass, his eyes as smoky as his voice. 'I'd give it all away in a heartbeat for one more night with you, darling.'

Nina nearly spilled the remainder of her wine. God, for an instant her mind had slipped a cog and she thought he actually meant it!

'Overextravagant compliments don't impress me,' she said repressively.

'"Was ever woman in this humour woo'd? Was ever woman in this humour won?"' he murmured, leaning his chin on his hand.

'Not when she remembers what the next line is,' she sparked back. '"I'll have her; but I will not keep her long."'

He threw back his head and laughed. 'Caught out! I should have expected it, knowing how much you like Shakespeare. It's one of the things we have in common.'

'Then you'd do better to avoid any more lines from *King Richard III*,' she told him, feeling a warmth in her belly that had nothing to do with the food and wine. So it hadn't been just an irresistible physical attraction of opposites! 'Unless you really *want* me to think of you as a villain.'

'I thought you already did.'

'Anyone who can cook the way you do can't be all bad.'

She regretted the impulsive reply as soon as it slipped out, but instead of seizing the opportunity to put her to the blush, he merely inclined his head in lazy acknowledgment of the compliment.

The cloudless warm day had turned into a crystal-clear cold night, and as Nina carried the dishes out to the kitchen and stacked them to soak for a while in the sink, Ryan rose with his glass of wine and strolled over towards the beckoning warmth of the fire.

When she came back into the room, he was lounging at ease on the hearth, propped up on one elbow as he toasted the long line of his back, his legs extended across the flokati rug, Zorro dozing in his favourite spot by the woodpile just beyond his feet.

'Come over and sit by the fire.' Ryan put his wineglass down to one side and held out his hand in a casual gesture of invitation.

Nina automatically extended her hand, gliding towards him with the blankness of a sleepwalker, but then she stumbled to a stop, her eyes widening as they fixed on the shaggy, cream woollen rug on which he was lying.

'Nina?' he murmured, the soft caress of her name echoing and re-echoing in her mind....

His nude body looked like polished teak in the firelight, smooth and sleek, bold in its arousal, the cloud of midnight hair in his groin a dark frame for the thick shaft that rose against his hard belly and nudged against her restless thighs. His mouth was as hot as the flames that bore mute witness to their passion as it seared across Nina's skin, leaving her swollen breasts glistening with moisture and her nipples engorged with fiery sweetness.

The thick rug generated a soft friction against her undulating back as he pressed her down against the unyielding floor, providing an erotic contrast to the sensual slide of his slick skin against hers, his entwining limbs moving over, under, around, between, seeking and finding every delicious pressure point in her eager woman's body.

His mouth moved to capture her wild cries, enrapturing her senses while his body ravished her with ruthless pleasure, his hands sliding down to cup her bottom and tilt her hips so that he could—

'Nina, aren't you going to sit down?'

Her soaring passion fell to earth with a crash as the scene telescoped back into her head. Ryan had lowered his hand and was sitting up, his eyes on her glazed face.

'Nina?' he repeated very gently, as if afraid of jolting her out of her seeming trance. 'What do you see?'

She couldn't answer, her jaw locked as she struggled to conceal her ragged emotions.

He stroked his hand across the shaggy rug, threading his fingers into the long, soft strands, drawing her fascinated gaze. 'Is it this rug? Does it remind you of something?' His voice lowered to a husky drawl, his fingers curling sensuously into the thick, wavy wool. 'We used to make love for hours on the big sheepskin rug at home. You loved being naked with me in the firelight, watching me make love to you with those gorgeous, sexy green eyes.

'Did you know you never close your eyes when you have an orgasm, Nina? Not until you've seen me climax, too. Are you remembering how incredibly arousing it is to watch each other in the throes of an orgasm? And when we made love in front of the fire, you always wanted it to be slow and easy so that it would last a long, long time.

Sometimes we even used to have fires in the middle of summer just for the sake of pleasuring ourselves with prolonged bouts of hot, sweaty sex interspersed with refreshing romps in the pool....'

He trailed off and a furious blush engulfed her, breaking the mesmerising spell of his evocative words. 'I'm tired. I want to go to bed,' she blurted.

'It's too early. You've just eaten. Come and sit by the fire where it's warm,' he murmured enticingly, patting the rug. 'You know you want to.'

That was the problem. 'I have to do the dishes—'

'I'll do them later. I created the mess. Let me clean it up. What's the matter, Nina? Afraid you won't be able to resist me? Why don't you come here and prove that you can?'

She was not fool enough to fall for that childish challenge, not when her feelings for him were anything but childish.

'I—I have some work to do.' She lifted her chin at his mocking expression of disbelief. 'I have someone picking up some commissions tomorrow. I'm sure you can keep yourself entertained—you seem to be doing pretty well at it so far,' she said tartly.

'Well, I was never one for solitary pleasures, but I'll give it a try,' he said blandly. 'If I have a problem, I'll be sure to use you as my inspiration.'

After another restless night of broken dreams, Nina was chagrined to wake up in a shaft of unruly sunlight and realise that she had overslept. She bounced out of bed and was surprised to find that, for once, she was up before Ryan.

She was sitting at the table eating her breakfast when he sleepily emerged, looking impossibly sexy in his rumpled work clothes, his hair frankly mussed, rasping his hand over his unshaven chin and generally acting like the man of the house.

'Morning, darling,' he greeted her, stooping to plant a leisurely kiss on her startled mouth before moving smartly out of striking distance to shake cereal into his bowl. 'What are we doing today?' he said, sliding into the chair opposite and raising amused eyebrows at her fulminating glare.

'*We?* I know what *I'm* doing,' she said through tingling lips. 'I have no idea what *your* plans might be.'

He grinned. 'Oh, I think you do. That's why you're looking at me like a scared rabbit.'

She refused to dignify that with an answer. 'You have work to do at Ray's—'

'He knows that my first priority is looking after you.'

'I don't *need* any looking after,' she gritted.

'That's a matter of opinion. It's going to be another lovely day,' he said, looking out the window, 'although that wind looks as if it might have a razor's edge. Do you have any more blankets, by the way? I was quite cold during the night.'

Had he been as restless as she was, and for the same reason? He couldn't have been—otherwise he would have wanted cold showers, not more blankets!

'In the other spare room. Help yourself,' Nina replied shortly. How could he talk about mundane things like the weather and blankets when there was so much unresolved between them? Every time they looked at each other, the air sizzled.

He kept up the innocuous patter over coffee and toast, and by the time there was a knock on the back door, Nina was on the verge of screaming.

Ryan paused, looking at her quizzically over his coffee cup. 'Are we expecting someone?'

That irritating 'we' again. 'That'll probably be George,' she said, dabbing the toast crumbs from her mouth as she got to her feet. 'He said he was coming over sometime today to collect the latest paintings for his book.'

Ryan put his cup down, pushing his chair back from the table to give himself a good view of the door. 'Ah, yes, the botanist you're doing those plant studies for. Ray says you've been working more closely with him recently.'

'Well, George likes to keep up with my progress. It's a good income for me, and I've always enjoyed painting plants and flowers.'

'He lives over by the reserve, doesn't he?'

'Only temporarily. He's a professor at Auckland University, spending a year's sabbatical here while he completes his research. He's already discovered a new species of native fern.'

'Bully for George,' he muttered, and watched her absently check the tuck of her green blouse in the waistband of her snug moleskins and smooth back her hair as she looked towards the door, all instinctively feminine actions that made his eyes narrow.

She caught his look and sensed trouble. 'I'll take him into the studio,' she told him hurriedly. 'If you wouldn't mind staying out of the way—this is business.'

'I'm glad to hear it,' he grunted, serving her a frisson of unease as she opened the door.

George Franklin had been extremely reserved when they first met at a working bee on one of the reserve's many bush tracks, but as their collaboration advanced, Nina had discovered that he was more preoccupied than deliberately aloof, and in the past couple of months their mutual liking had warmed into comfortable friendship. Nina felt no excitement in his company, but she liked him and lately had been wondering if she should react to his tentative hints that he would like their friendship to ripen into something more.

Now, as he greeted her with his slightly abstracted smile

and a warm kiss on her cheek, she wondered how on earth she could ever have considered him in the light of a romantic attachment. He was only a few years older than her, and good-looking in a boyish kind of way, with sandy hair, freckled face and golden-brown eyes, but there was nothing about him that would ever call to her soul.

She stiffened as Ryan came up behind her, sliding his arm around her waist and drawing her firmly back against him, his other hand extended politely to the other man. 'Hello, George. Ryan Flint.' He gave the automatically proffered hand a white-knuckled shake that caused the professor's eyes to widen.

'Don't leave him standing on the doorstep, darling,' he said in Nina's ear, accompanying his words with a chiding nip of her soft lobe.

'Would you like me to make you a coffee, George, while Nina is showing you the paintings?' He gave the disconcerted visitor a charmingly affable smile. 'I think you'll be pleased with what she's done—Nina has a real feeling for the work. In fact, she's one of the most gifted botanical artists I've seen in a long while. She makes a very good argument for the superiority of botanical art over photographic reproduction.'

George looked as if he was about to cut in with something condescending, so Nina conquered her stunned reaction to Ryan's lavish praise and rushed to explain.

'Ryan is an art dealer, George,' she said, surreptitiously pinching the encompassing arm until she was allowed to wriggle free. 'He owns the Pacific Rim Galleries.'

'Really?' George looked warily from Nina's flustered face to Ryan's formidably square-jawed expression. 'I've heard of them, of course, but...well, I'm afraid I don't know much about modern art—'

'And I don't know much about botany,' Ryan said smoothly. 'But I do know that some of those paintings of

Nina's are good enough to be framed as individual works.
Have you considered conducting a gallery showing in con-
junction with the publication of your book? It's a very spe-
cialised area and I know academic publications are usually
slid into the market without any fanfare, but there's no
reason it couldn't be a success if it was expertly organised.
I know for a fact there are a number of notable botanical-
art collectors in Australasia.

'If you had your book launch in an art gallery, it would
not only be good publicity for your book, but it would give
Nina—and you—a wider audience recognition. Not to men-
tion the potential additional profit for you both, of course.'

'You really think I could do that?' George looked much
intrigued, and Nina was incensed when they went through
to her studio and he skimped on his normally laborious
study of each painting in order to spend most of his visit
brainstorming with Ryan about the possibility of a showing
at Pacific Rim.

In spite of her best efforts to distance herself from Ryan's
constant smiling glances and give the impression that the
casual 'darlings' with which he peppered her during conversation were merely an arty affectation, by the time
George left she knew that she wouldn't be getting any more
tentative invitations to picnics in the reserve.

Sure enough, there was no friendly buss on the cheek at
the door, just a rueful wave. Then Ryan insisted on helping
him carry the paintings out to his muddy station wagon so
he would only have to make one trip, leaving Nina quietly
fretting in the kitchen, gnawing her lip when she peeped
out the window and saw Ryan talking expressively before
offering a few comradely pats on the shoulder in farewell.

'How dare you take over like that!' Nina said to him
when he came back inside. 'I told you to stay out of the
way.'

'I was only trying to give both your careers a boost,' he

said piously. 'What's wrong with that? I thought you'd be pleased I was so friendly to your friend.'

'*Friendly!*' Nina had another word for it. 'What were you saying to him out there at the end?' she demanded.

'I was telling him to look for another woman as you're already taken. By me.'

'You didn't tell him like *that?*' she screeched.

'Well, I put it a bit more tactfully, of course,' he lied. 'Don't look so horrified. He wouldn't have been any good for you as a lover anyway. You need someone earthy, someone who has sensual appetites to match your own. And he knows nothing about art, for goodness' sake—and you're an artist! What would you talk about out of bed? You need someone who understands your moods, your passions, your frustrations.

'Face it, Nina, you need *me*. You'll never find a lover more perfectly attuned to your desires, and the bonus is— I'm right here for the taking!'

CHAPTER EIGHT

NINA plunged full tilt down the steep, uneven dirt track, clutching at the slender, peeling trunks of the kanuka trees on either side of the narrow trail in an attempt slow her reckless momentum as she approached the bottom of the hill and finally shot out into the open grove to be brought up short by Ryan's open arms.

He staggered as she hit his chest, and they almost fell onto the carpet of leaf mould in a wild tangle of limbs.

'Dammit, Nina, you should be more careful. You could have broken your neck,' he said as he steadied her briefly before firmly putting her away from him.

'Sorry, I started off a little fast and once I got going I just couldn't seem to stop myself,' she said, panting, her body still thrilling from the forceful impact with his.

'Believe me, I'm familiar with the feeling,' he said with involuntary roughness.

Nina glided him a look from under her lashes. 'Then why fight it?' She had been trying for three days to needle him into action, and to her frustration all he seemed to want to do was *talk*. She began brushing imaginary dust from the open neck of her blouse with fluttering little strokes of her fingers, even flicking open another button to reveal more of her cleavage.

His hand snapped around her wrist. 'What do you think you're doing?'

'Making myself more comfortable.' She gave him a look of wide-eyed innocence.

'You can take it off altogether if you like,' he clipped. 'It's not going to make any difference.'

'Why, because you've seen it all before?' she taunted him.

'No, because you can trust me not to take advantage of your more foolish impulses.'

'What if I *want* you to take advantage of them?' she declared recklessly.

'You want me to grab you and throw you to the ground and have sex with you right here in the dirt in the middle of a public reserve?'

She flushed.

'Because I am physically capable of it, Nina,' he said, gesturing angrily down at himself. 'But I'm *not* capable of pretending afterwards that it hasn't happened. When and if you want us to be lovers again, then you have to be prepared to face the consequences.' He turned and continued along the track that would bring them out at the eastern edge of the scenic reserve.

'What consequences?' she cried in frustration, dragging him to a halt by the sleeve of his shirt. 'I've admitted I remember the beginning of our affair. How can I be expected to face what I still can't remember? If it's so important, why don't you *tell* me?'

'Because just *telling* you about your past life won't make it any more real to you if you can't attach any *feelings* to the memories. Although you thought you'd forgotten I existed, you still had the *emotional* memory of me, which started you on the road to remembering.'

This time, it was Nina's turn to walk away. 'You're implying I have some sort of *control* over this thing.'

He caught up with her easily on the narrow track. 'I'm only pointing out that you seem more afraid of remembering than you do of forgetting,' he said quietly. 'Maybe that fall on the ferry completed a process that had already begun, and hitting your head provided your mind with a perfectly logical opportunity for you to dissociate yourself from the problem period in your life.'

'My problem period being my entire relationship with *you!*' she said bitterly. 'In other words, you're saying you don't believe I have amnesia at all.'

'Oh, I have no doubt that you do—just not the brain-injury kind. And I think you subconsciously know that, which is why you've been avoiding doctors.'

'I avoid doctors because I had enough of medical experts while Gran was dying! It was a truly horrible time. If I was looking for a period of my life I wanted to dissociate from, surely it would have been *that* one!'

They walked the rest of the road in uneasy silence, but when they got back to the house, Ryan went straight into his room and came back carrying a plastic folder of photographs.

'You missed them when you frisked my bag—they were in the side compartment,' he said, placing them on the bookshelf. 'I'll leave them here for when you're ready to look at them.'

His caution was like a red rag to a bull. 'I'm ready now!' declared Nina, determined to prove that she wasn't entirely a cringing coward. 'Are you going to tell me what they are?' she asked as she sat at the table and took them out of the folder.

'Why don't you just look at them and ask me questions?' He straddled a chair and folded his arms along the curved back.

There were twenty in all—glossy, sunny photographs that showed no hints of any lurking unhappiness—mostly of Ryan and Nina together, but there were a few pictures of a big, white, double-storeyed, Mediterranean-style house, a large swimming pool surrounded by clusters of lush palms and of people she didn't know, including one of a little boy not yet out of nappies, dressed in cute denim overalls and sitting astride a push-along wooden horse, his curly black hair standing up all over his head, his blue eyes twinkling with laughter at the camera. Nina barely glanced at that one, her eyes blanking with disinterest as she pushed it quickly aside under the others.

Ryan watched her action with eyes that were bleak with pain. Deliberately, he fished out the photo she had just discarded and fingered it as he asked, 'Any questions?'

Nina's heart jerked with dread, and she reshuffled the photos until the top one displayed the picture of the Mediterranean house. 'I get a strong sense of deja vu about the places and those pictures of you and I—I remember doing some of those things with you—'

'But you don't remember any of the other people?'

He was still fingering the photograph, so Nina didn't look at him. She didn't want to start talking about the people and certainly wasn't interested in other people's babies....

She shook her head. 'Most of them are just faces, except for Katy. I suppose she's studying in America now.'

For a brief instant, his face lit up with pride. 'She's getting top marks and has already had several good job offers in the States.'

Out of the corner of her eye, she saw Ryan slip the picture he was holding into the breast pocket of his white shirt. Through the thin linen she could see only the vague, shadowy outline of an image.

She relaxed and smiled at him, but he didn't smile back. She put the photos back in their folder and began to slide them across to him.

'Keep them. You never know. Each time you look at them you might be able to build on that feeling of familiarity.' He got up, running his fingers through his hair in a weary gesture that exposed the edge of the healing red wound on his upper temple.

'You really should see about getting someone to take out those stitches,' she said. 'Dave said they shouldn't need to stay in for more than a week.'

'Has it been only a week?' Ryan murmured. 'Somehow it seems a lot longer than that.'

Nina agreed. It felt like a lifetime!

He gave himself a mental shake and looked down at her, his mouth curving humourlessly. 'Actually, I *am* seeing someone right now. I'll get the hot water and towel while you sterilise the scissors.'

'You don't expect me to take them out!'

'Why not? Dave said it was so straightforward I could almost do it myself. Just snip and pull.'

Nina shuddered, but her protests were ruthlessly overridden and she soon found herself bending over him, the hot scissors betraying a fine tremble in her hand as they approached his forehead.

She hesitated, half straightening. 'I don't want to hurt you....' she worried.

'On that spectacular piece of irony, you can proceed,' he told her harshly. 'I doubt that you could hurt me more than you already have!'

She gasped. 'That's not fair—'

'Life isn't fair, darling. Haven't you figured that out yet? Now stop torturing me, dammit, and just get it over with.'

She did, with the utmost delicacy—and wincing all the way.

'There, you see?' He took the scissors from her nerveless hand when she had finished and dabbed a piece of clean gauze against the scar. 'You did fine. It just goes to prove that sometimes the anticipation of pain is worse than the actual pain itself...even when we're inflicting it on someone else from the best possible motives,' he added huskily.

On that cryptic note he departed to see if Ray's new

balcony rail had arrived, and Nina didn't see him for the rest of the afternoon.

And, wretchedly, she missed him. Too restless to settle down to her study of the final set of specimen plants that George had brought with him and determined not to traipse next door to gawp at him fixing Ray's rail like a lovesick schoolgirl, Nina was reduced to doing housework and subsequently was in a bad mood when Ryan came back with the news that the five Peterson children were building a huge pyre of driftwood on the beach, and they were invited to take a blanket along and watch the bonfire when the pyre was ceremoniously torched after dark.

'Look at those clouds coming in. And the wind is getting up, too. I bet it's going to rain,' Nina said dampeningly, but Ryan was as eager as a boy, confiding that he hadn't been to a beach bonfire since he was a child, and gradually she found herself infected with his enthusiasm to the extent of fossicking out miniatures of liqueur—given to her by one of her boarders as a farewell gift—to toast the blaze.

Later, bundled up in layers of clothing and huddled against Ryan's side under the mohair blanket, his heavy arm cuddled around her shoulders, Nina conceded to the Peterson children in a voice hoarse from a raucous sing-along that, yes, it could well qualify as the best bonfire ever, any time in history, anywhere on the planet.

Ryan rewarded her for her graciousness with a nip of the peach schnapps, which was Ray's contribution to the adult entertainment, and pounded her laughingly on the back when the fiery spirit seared her throat and brought tears to her eyes.

As the interlaced cone of wood collapsed inwards on itself in a shower of sparks that whirled up into the night sky, the youngest Peterson, a plump toddler, made a sudden dash past Nina towards the fascinating embers.

Ryan lunged forward and scooped the errant child back

to the safety of the blanket, balancing him on his out-stretched legs and warning him in a deep, gentle voice that that wasn't a wise thing to do. Nina stiffened and shrank away as Rosalie Peterson rushed over to pick up her son. 'Oh, dear, I'm sorry,' she said with a rueful smile at Nina. 'I know you don't like being bothered by the little ones, but you know how toddlers are!'

'No, actually, I don't,' Nina said stiltedly, turning her face back to the fire, aware of the sudden tension in the body next to her. Suddenly, the euphoria of the evening drained abruptly away and she was anxious to leave. 'It's getting late. I'm tired...I think I'll go back to the house,' she muttered, scrambling to her feet and blocking out the chorus of voices as she offered a falsely casual goodnight and hurried away.

The farther Nina got from the glow of the bonfire the colder she felt and she wrapped her arms around herself to conserve her body heat as her sneakers swished through the frigid sand. Suddenly, a blanket dropped over her shoulders and Ryan was there, striding silently alongside her with Zorro a panting shadow at his heels.

'You didn't have to leave, as well,' she ventured guiltily. Kicking out the embers and burying them in sand was part of the fun of having a bonfire.

'I did if I wanted to be with you,' he said. 'Although it's a shame to miss the—'

There was a booming detonation behind them and Nina whirled around with a small scream.

'—fireworks,' Ryan finished as an incandescent white light shot into the sky, followed by successive balls of ex-ploding white sparks emitting high-pitched screams. Zorro, far from being upset by the cacophony, immediately dashed back to the excitement. 'Chas said they were left over from last year's Guy Fawkes—'

He suddenly noticed Nina crouched on the sand, shaking,

her face buried against her knees, her hands pressed over her ears.

'Nina—what's wrong?'

He had to kneel down beside her to hear her reedy reply.

'I don't—I hate fireworks. I'm sorry, I know it's silly, but I just can't bear them.'

'It's all right, we're well away from them. They can't hurt you—'

'I know that, I *know* that. I just…the noise, the smoke of them, it makes me feel sick. I don't know why—' She cringed as there was another bang.

'Don't you?' His arm came around her, pulling her into his side so that she could bury her tear-stained face in his chest, crushing her shuddering body to his as if he could absorb her paralysing fear. '*Don't you*, Nina?' he asked with fierce urgency that reached to the core of her being.

'I…no…yes…yes…my mother,' she gasped against his pounding heart. 'Since she died in that explosion…I've hated Guy Fawkes…hated seeing all those flashes, like the one that killed Mummy and Laurie.'

'Your *mother?*' She felt his heart slow for a fraction of a second, then accelerate even faster. 'But you didn't see the flash, Nina,' he reminded her. 'You said you were playing next door at the neighbours'.'

'But…no…' She lifted her face, a ghostly glimmer in the darkness, illuminated by pulsating flashes of colour from the far end of the beach. 'No…' Her stunned wet eyes sought his, her hands curling into his black sweater. 'No, *no*—I wasn't. Isn't that odd? I—I didn't remember it until now, but I *wasn't* next door. I was only *supposed* to be. It was my sixth birthday and Mummy was going to ice the cake she'd made me. She told me to go outside and play on the seesaw, but I didn't think it was fair that Laurie was allowed to see and not me, so I crept back. I was peeping in the crack of the kitchen door when, when—oh, God, I saw it happen…I saw it happen!' She shuddered, welcoming his suffocating grip.

'There was a big flash—I was knocked over. The door, I think it came off…and there was smoke in there and sparks from the ceiling and everything was broken and Mummy and Laurie weren't there any more, so I ran next door to get on the seesaw so Mummy wouldn't know I'd been bad…because maybe it happened because I was bad!

'I just rocked and rocked on that seesaw until Mrs Petley saw me and took me inside, and the fire engines came and then Gran and Gramps, and nobody ever asked what I'd seen because they all just assumed I'd been in the Petleys' garden. It was even in the papers—and it was always what Gran told people. I grew up thinking it was true. But it wasn't. And all this time I repressed it. God.' The childish agony was in her voice. 'I remember being so scared everyone would think it was my *fault*….'

He cupped his hand on the back of her head. 'It wasn't your fault, Nina.'

'But she was making my cake—'

'It wasn't your fault. A heater was faulty. That wasn't your fault.' There was heartfelt despair in his voice as he tried to persuade her. 'You can't always control what happens to other people or protect them from unseen danger. Accidents happen, and there's nothing you can do about it. You just have to accept it.'

'At least now I know why I react so badly to fireworks and sudden loud noises.' She risked a look back along the beach to where the moving figures were silhouetted by a brilliant emerald green glow in the sand. 'I wonder why I suddenly remembered this time?'

'Perhaps because that particular memory isn't the pre-eminent threat it used to be. Perhaps because tonight when it happened, you were with someone you—you instinctively trusted to understand.'

'I'm c-cold!' Nina was racked with violent shivers as she knelt in the sand, her cramped limbs feeling numb under her clothing. 'Oh, God, why am I so cold...?'

'Because it's freezing out here and you've given yourself a shock.' Ryan wrapped her tightly in the blanket and stood up, holding her swaddled body high against his chest as he carried her over the sand and up the bank to the house.

Once inside, he set her down by the fire and rubbed at her arms and back through the fabric, but she still couldn't stop her shivering. She fought her arms free of the mohair folds and wrapped them around him, going on tiptoe so that she could press her face into the curve of his neck, into his warm male flesh.

'Ryan...oh, Ryan.' She felt grief, the old remembered pain mixing with a new and confusing swirl of emotion. This man was someone that she feared, that she knew in her heart had the power to hurt her, and yet she wanted him, needed him, needed the strength and support he represented and, yes, the joy, too. 'Hold me,' she whispered frantically to him, as he had once begged her. Her mouth opened against his throat, her tongue stroking, tasting him, savouring the remembered ecstasy.

'Nina—you're still freezing. You should take a hot shower...' he began hoarsely.

'No...I want you to warm me up!' She let her head tip back, her arms sliding over his shoulders, her hands linking at the nape of his neck, her spiky-damp lashes framing green eyes that glowed with turbulent passion.

He groaned, the blanket falling in hushed folds to the floor as his hands lifted from her back, hovering away from her sides as if he dared not touch her. 'How do you expect me to do that?'

She licked her parted lips, glossing them with inviting moisture. 'You know how....' she said huskily. She half lowered her pale eyelids, giving her upturned face a look of slumberous sensuality even as her body vibrated with tension.

His hands settled convulsively at her waist, his thumbs pushing up against her lower ribs. 'You don't know what you want from me,' he said in a strained voice.

'Yes, I do,' she countered, arching her spine so that her breasts moved against his chest. 'I'm asking you to make love to me.' Her hands trailed down over his chest and up under his sweater to find the nipples that she knew were sensitive, pressing against his shirt. 'I thought that was what you wanted, too,' she murmured, scratching at them with her fingernails.

With a rough curse, he caught at her hands, pulling them roughly out from under the fine wool and manacling them together. Nina retaliating by lifting one knee, sliding it up the inner seam of his trousers until her thigh pressed into the notch between his legs, rubbing against an exciting hardness.

'Come on, Ryan, there's no reason to hold back any more,' she urged throatily, the hot and cold shivers thrilling her body intensifying the urgency of her desire. 'Remind me what a fantastic lover you are.'

He bent his head and crushed the provocative words back into her mouth in a long, mind-bending, soul-savaging kiss. Then, with shocking suddenness, he broke it off, resting his hard forehead against hers as they both struggled for breath, and he fought for control.

'Go and have your shower, Nina,' he ordered thickly. 'For both our sakes. You need to warm up, take the edge off a shattering experience so you can really think about what you're doing.'

She let him push her away, but she felt his shuddering reluctance and knew that she hadn't lost the battle.

'I'm not shattered,' she said softly. 'Maybe I should be, but I'm not. I feel lighter, freer. If anything, I'm thinking more clearly about myself than I have for a long time.' She crossed her arms, gripping the bottom of her fleece jumper and pulled it swiftly over her head, taking with it her woollen skivvy and nylon camisole, leaving her upper body bare but for a lacy emerald bra, a shade darker than her sultry eyes.

She shook her clinging clothes down off her arms, aware of her breasts shimmering enticingly against the low-cut scalloping of lace. The hot caress of his gaze and the quickened tenor of his ragged breathing increased the tempo of her own pulse. She touched the tiny, pearl-centred bow between the wired cups, drawing his attention to the insecurity of the catch, then toyed with one strap, running her finger back and forth underneath it before teasing it slowly off her shoulder.

'I'll go and have a shower because it seems *you* need time to decide what you really want,' she said throatily, doing the same slow tease with the other strap and bringing her arms forward to wrap across her soft abdomen, deepening the shadowy crevice between her creamy breasts, her fingers splaying over her silky-bare sides. 'But I'll be thinking of you while I'm in there, thinking and wanting, and waiting....'

Nina tilted her face in voluptuous appreciation as the hot water poured down over the top of her head, streaming over her eyes and ears and mouth, rendering her blind, deaf and dumb to the rest of the world. She didn't know how long she'd been in there and she no longer cared, her mind floating blissfully free, her steaming body massaged by the tingling needles of spray.

The only warning she had was a faint fan of cool air across her back, and then a big body crowded into the stall behind her, joining her under the wide stream of water, a thick arm snaking around her waist and pulling her back against a nude, hairy male body, already powerfully aroused. Sharp teeth sank into her wet shoulder and a strong hand came around to knead her breasts as his thick shaft settled along the cleft in her bottom. She wriggled her hips and the hand on her breast contracted.

'I knew you'd come,' she whispered.

'We're both going to come, babe.' The furry growl in her ear made her insides turn to warm honey. 'Hand me the soap.'

'I've already—'

'Shut up and hand me the soap.' His order carried a sexual aggressiveness that she found intensely exciting. She had driven him to this and now she was more than willing to accept that she was no longer in control.

She had already soaped herself, but not like this...never like this...not with such intimate attention to detail, not as if each individual pore and singing nerve ending deserved special cleansing. He sucked the water off the lobes of her ears and the sides of her neck in between his soft nips across her shoulders, his soapy fingers slipping and sliding around her aching breasts, returning again and again to her nipples, tugging and massaging until she was panting and squirming in her efforts to turn around and touch him with the same intimacy.

He wouldn't let her, and deliciously frustrated by her enforced helplessness, she reached back to grip his hairy flanks, her fingers stroking the long, flexing muscles as he worked his body against hers, undulating his hips so that she was in no doubt of his sexual intent. Her head fell back against his shoulder and he roughly nudged her chin around so that he could capture her mouth, his tongue darting between her teeth in the same rhythm that drove the rotating thrust of his hips.

'Open your legs,' he whispered roughly into her mouth, his hands circling around her soapy navel, massaging ever lower, pressing down over the inside of her thighs until they parted for him, allowing his soap-slick fingers to crowd into the steamy space and play over the secret folds in her skin, exploring her readiness and finding the sweet kernel of budded desire.

Her fingers clawed into his flanks at the drenching burst of pleasure that pulsed hotly against his fingers. 'Oh, Ryan...'

'Yeah, babe, I know.' She almost sobbed as his magical touch left her, but it was only to grab her wrists and place her flat hands against the steamy wall in front of her, then he was gripping her hips again, nudging her ankles farther apart with his and lifting her to receive a powerful thrust that made her cry out as she felt him touch her womb, her back arching to ease his passage into her swollen tissues, her forehead falling forward against her hands as he withdrew and pushed in again...and again, higher and deeper and faster, one arm hooking around the front of her pelvis to steady her for his quickening thrusts, his other hand sweeping up and down the supple bow of spine to stroke the lush, round globes of her quivering bottom.

The hot water pounded down over their violently surging bodies, heightening the wild, wet thrills, and Nina gave herself up to the anarchy of pure passion. She felt Ryan's teeth grate against her shoulder-blade, his increasingly erratic rhythm forcing her closer and closer to the wall until her swollen nipples were jarring against the cool, slippery wallboard with each dynamic thrust of his hips.

She uttered a tiny choking cry as she approached a pinnacle of sensation only to have the prize snatched from her grasp when Ryan suddenly withdrew and spun her around so that it was now her spine flat to the wall, her thighs urged up around his waist by his rough hands as he bluntly surged back into her welcoming body, grunting in triumph at the slick parting of her folds, shuddering as she instantly contracted around his pulsing hardness.

'I love to see you watching me when you come apart. I want to watch you, too....' Intoxicating urgency was in his voice, in his burning blue eyes as they locked with her wide-eyed gaze. Her legs tightened around his waist, freeing his hands to cup her breasts, his thumbs pushing on the stiff nipples as if he was pressing buttons he knew were wired directly to all the pleasure centres of her body.

At the same moment, his eyes still fixed on her fast-dilating pupils, he arched back slightly, allowing the full force of the hot spray to splash down on the point where their bodies joined, and Nina instantly went over the edge, convulsing violently in his arms, her keening cry of ecstatic surrender destroying his attempt to hold back long enough for her to finish, catapulting him into a vicious paroxysm of guttural pleasure that sent a ripple of aftershocks cascading through her senses.

Exhausted, they slumped against the wall, but when Nina delicately tried to disengage herself, Ryan muttered a protest, his legs buckling as he carried her down with him to the metal floor of the shower box.

'Ryan...' she squeaked as he laid her on her back in the shallow pool of draining water, bending her knees to fit within the box so that he could crawl between them.

'Did you think we'd finished?' he growled as he knelt over her, the water bouncing off his shielding back, creating a halo of fine droplets around the back of his head. The Angel of Unrelenting Pleasure, she thought deliriously. 'No way, babe....'

She was laughing, not really believing him, and her eyes widened as he bent eagerly to his task, his mouth and hands exploring everywhere he hadn't already touched and tasted, and very shortly he was proving himself capable all over again. More than capable, Nina thought dreamily when it was all over.

'The water's cold,' she announced suddenly, even though she didn't feel in the least bit chilled any more.

He tipped his head back up into the spray, the movement grinding his heavy, sated body delightfully against her ravished femininity.

'So it is.' He reached up with one hand to turn off the shower, creating another wonderful, crushing thrill in her loins. Then she realised that the water was lapping surprisingly high around her shoulders and felt an odd tugging under her left hip.

She started giggling uncontrollably and he looked down at her, enchanted by the sight of her lovely eyes filled with the familiar dancing mischief that he had feared he might never see again.

'Either someone else is in here with us or I'm lying on the plug hole. I think I'm going to have a very large love bite on my bottom,' she said, giggling again.

His eyes gleamed in answering appreciation. 'This I've got to see,' he murmured wickedly, hauling her up and roughly towelling them both before hustling her across the hall into his bedroom. 'The doctor is ready for you now, my dear,' he intoned with a leer, then tumbled her face down onto the bed.

Her irrepressible giggles were stifled in his pillow. 'What do you think, Doctor?' she said when he seemed to be taking an inordinate amount of time to make his diagnosis.

'Hmmm...' She felt his finger trace a teasing circle on her flushed cheek. 'Definitely treatable. I think Dr Flint has the perfect remedy for this, to be applied regularly and often....' Suddenly, a warm, wet tongue was anointing the spot.

'Ryan...' Her feeble chuckle of protest turned huskily eager as his tongue wandered farther afield. 'Ryan...'

They made love again, this time languorously, lingering over each soft touch and slow kiss, and when it was over they lay contentedly in each other's arms.

'Bring back any memories?' he murmured, and Nina kissed the hard shoulder that pillowed her head.

'Some...'

His lips drifted over her hair. 'Good memories?'

'Oh, yes...all good.' She smiled against his skin, absently stroked the jagged scar that streaked like a lightning bolt up the side of his thigh.

'I was in an accident,' he said suddenly, and her fingers faltered, then moved up to rest on his unblemished chest as she shifted her head to look up at him.

'Before I met you?' she asked nervously. Her memories of him had not included a scar on his leg.

'No, after.'

'You mean after I left?'

'No, it was while we were together.'

The careful neutrality of his voice made her afraid to delve further. She was happy and relaxed. She didn't want anything to spoil this precious idyll. She suspected that it was only the eye of the storm, but she wanted to enjoy it while she could. 'Well, I still think you're sexy, battle scars and all,' she said lightly.

'I think you're sexy, too.' He stroked her stomach, looking down, his finger tracking a long, curving line towards her hip. 'Even with *your* battle scars.'

She looked down at the faint tracery of thin silver lines on her belly. 'They're not scars,' she automatically denied.

'Then what are they?' he persisted softly.

She pushed his hand away and squirmed her hips towards him so that her stomach was pressed against his, concealing the sight of the inexplicable flaws. 'Can't you leave a woman her vanity?'

'"Vanity, thy name is woman!"' he quoted, not pressing the point.

'Hamlet said "frailty", not "vanity",' she corrected. 'And I'm not frail—I'm a lusty young lass!'

She had made him laugh and the shadowed moment passed, and as the long hours of the night slipped away, they slept and woke and whispered and made love, and in the morning they breakfasted together as lovers do, and the only time they touched on anything remotely serious was when Nina said, 'I had nothing to do with your money going missing, Ryan. There *has* to be some other explanation. Whatever else I may be, I know I'm not a thief!'

He merely nodded thoughtfully and changed the subject, but she didn't allow herself to believe the matter was laid finally to rest. Ryan hadn't become an extremely wealthy man by forgiving his debts.

Later that day when she took Ray's lunch over to him and had to run the gauntlet of his shrewd comments and knowing chuckles, she took the opportunity to phone Karl, disappointed to discover that he was out on a sales call and not answering his cell phone. She had to content herself with leaving a stilted message on his answerphone, not sure who else might listen to the recording.

'Karl, it's Nina. I just wanted you to know that Ryan Flint has turned up here at Puriri Bay. I—he's staying with me—we need to talk—please call me.'

She had expected that sometime in the next few days Ray would call her over to the phone, so it was a shock to see Karl coming through the door from the deck the very next afternoon.

He was no longer the scruffy surfer he once had been. His shoulder-length blond hair was shiny clean and caught back in a trendy ponytail, his eyes clear of drugs, his shoulders square under the sharp threads, although he still sported the deeply tanned face that was the legacy of his love of the beach, along with his trademark semishaven chin.

'Where is he?' were the first words out of his mouth.

Her stunned greeting died on her lips. 'He and Zorro are taking a walk on the beach,' she said equally curtly. 'Karl, what are you doing here?'

'What do you think I'm doing? You wanted to talk. Here I am,' he answered sullenly. 'I suppose you've got your memory back. When did he turn up?'

'Some things I remember…not all. Ryan arrived a week ago. He's been helping me—'

'I bet he has,' he said snidely. 'A *week?* Are you sleeping with him again?' She blushed and he punched his fist into his palm. 'God, Nina, you were *happy* again—you didn't need him any more. You were doing great by yourself. You said you'd rediscovered your artistic soul! I kept him away for *you,* it was all for *you!* And now you're just going to let him walk back into your life like nothing happened? You've been apart for the nine months, but now… *God*— now you're *cohabiting* again,' he threw at her. 'You know what that means? It means now you'll have to wait *another* two years if you want to get a divorce—'

'A divorce!' It hit her like a thunderclap and she staggered, reaching blindly out for a chair into which she collapsed on unsteady legs. 'A *divorce?* I thought—he said we'd been living together, but… We got *married?*'

Karl looked equally thunderstruck by her shock. 'Three months after you met—'

'Ryan and I are *husband and wife?*' The wall in her mind was beginning to tilt, threatening to crash down on her, pulverise her beneath its full, crushing weight, and nightmarishly Nina found herself helpless to run.

Karl erupted in a fluent streak of curses. 'You mean you *hadn't* remembered? And he hasn't *told* you? *Any* of it?' Her white-faced silence said it all and he swore again, but with a strong undercurrent of bewilderment thickening his angry voice. 'What in the *hell* does he think he's playing at?' he snarled. But before she could ask him any more questions, he had spun on his heel and flung himself back out the door.

Nina was frozen to her seat. Two years. The two years that had been blocked out of her mind for so long had been the years during which she had met, loved *and married* Ryan Flint. She stared down at her hands...her bare hands. Something was missing. Something she had been used to seeing. Once there had been a wedding ring on that finger. *Once...*

Like an old woman, she got up and moved with arthritic stiffness down to the laundry where she opened the deep, ceiling-high linen closet. After dragging over a small stepladder, she went on tiptoe to the highest shelf and reached in to pull out a dusty leather satchel. It had been stuffed into her backpack when she arrived on the island. She had never opened it. She had thrust it into the back of the closet and never looked at it from that day to this, never even thought of it, blocked it out of her mind as surely as her memories. Now she took it into her bedroom and laid it on her coverlet, reaching for the dusty brass clasp with shaking fingers.

Photographs. Wedding photographs—a shaft of heat stopping memories of a simple ceremony in a beautiful little wooden church. A set of keys. Personal papers—her passport and birth certificate and...and a notarised certificate of marriage between Ryan Liam Flint and Nina Joan Dowling. And, wrapped in a handkerchief decorated with tiny teddy bears, one wedding ring, plain gold, eighteen carat, symbol of faith between a man and a woman, symbol of love and hope and shared dreams for the future....

And, finally, there was money. Bundles and bundles of money, rubber-banded together in compact stacks of large and small denominations. Untraceable used bills. *Ryan's money*, his missing cash float—although to Nina's sick shame it looked nowhere near the amount he had mentioned.

She snapped out of her dazed lethargy, batting away the questions that buzzed at her like a swarm of painfully stinging wasps. Karl—he had been so angry—where had he been going?

She ran outside to look along the beach, her stomach twisting into knots as she saw that her foster-brother had accosted Ryan and Zorro halfway down the sand and a heated debate was going on, complete with waving arms and jabbing fingers.

Suddenly, there was a violent flurry of movement, and Nina was horrified to see the two men physically slugging it out, an excited Zorro darting in and out of their feet.

Leaping off the deck, she dashed towards the beach, screaming both their names. Karl half turned to look at her, and in that unguarded instant, Ryan viciously charged him, catching him midsection with his lowered shoulder and carrying him heavily down onto the sand where they rolled over and over, grappling and punching while Zorro growled and made lightning forays to nip at their flailing legs.

'Stop it, you two! For God's sake, stop it!' Nina screamed, reaching them just as Ryan gained ascendancy, straddling the younger man and swinging a heavy fist, snapping Karl's head sideways on the sand. As he lifted his fist again, Nina caught his arm with both hands, twisting it with all her strength to wrench him away from her foster-brother. 'What do you think you're doing? Are you trying to *kill* him?'

'No, just teach him a lesson he won't forget,' Ryan ground out, ripping his sleeve out of her grasp, falling back panting on the sand as he saw with bitter eyes that her horrified concern was all for his opponent.

Karl was sitting up, his hand going to a rapidly swelling mouth streaming with blood, and Nina automatically felt in her jeans pocket for the paint rag she always tucked there while she was working, making a pad out of it as she dropped to her knees.

'You didn't have to hit him so hard.' She couldn't look at Ryan—at her *husband*—the man she had promised to love, honour and keep and, yes—she recalled the words of the traditional ceremony with bittersweet clarity—even *obey*...and then had deserted, *stolen* from, blithely wiped his existence from her mind....

'Get out of the way, Nina,' Ryan threatened, rolling to his feet. 'This is between me and him! We're going to settle the score once and for all.'

The eye of the storm had moved relentlessly on, and now Nina was once more battered by an emotional hurricane. God, he was such a proud man. How he must have *hated* her for humiliating him!

'I can't,' she said fiercely, still unable to look at him, concentrating on cradling Karl's head and pressing the pad gently against his split mouth, already puffed up to twice its size. 'Whatever's the matter, violence isn't the way to resolve it.'

It occurred to her that on past occasions Karl was quite capable of allowing himself to be beaten up if it meant causing more trouble for Ryan. He might think the temporary suffering worth the malicious opportunity to have Ryan charged with a serious assault. She couldn't risk that happening, not if she wanted to salvage anything of her marriage. If the only way to protect Ryan from Karl's malice was to protect Karl, then that was what she would do.

'Ryan, he told me I'm your wife—what he'd done. But I won't let you hurt him.' She finally forced herself to look up at him, but he was already turning his back.

'*The hell with you, then. The hell with you both!*' he

snarled, his words corrosive with bitterness, and she watched, shattered, as he walked away. She had expected him to stand his ground; she had never, ever expected him to simply give up. It wasn't in his nature.

He should have been able to depend on her loyalty and instead he must think that she had given her first loyalty to Karl—would always favour the bonds of childhood over the vows of marriage. She scrambled up, intending to go after him, to explain—

A clumsy hand on her arm stopped her as Karl swayed to his feet, holding the pad against his mouth. 'Wait—'

'But I have to go to him.' At least he was heading back to the house, she thought, watching the lean figure scale the bank with the little dog. Surely he must expect that Nina would follow—but only if she had decided that he was more important to her than the foster-brother who had betrayed them both.

'All right.' Karl's hand tightened. 'But first you have to listen to me. Please—it's important. To me—to you…and to *him*.'

That stayed her. She looked at him with sad eyes that made his tanned skin pale under the reddening contusions.

'I know…I'm despicable,' he said jerkily. 'He was right not to trust me. Katy and I—that would have been a bust anyway. It was like, you know, an ego trip for me. I got off on having her treat me like I was some kind of subversive hero. As much of a big shot as her brother.' He spoke in sharp, staccato bursts, pushing the confession out. 'But I wasn't, and he knew that. All he had to do was goad me into overplaying my hand and he knew I'd crash and burn. I was bitter over that, and you know how good I am about carrying a grudge—I even refused to come to your wedding.

'I was glad when you disappeared, and seeing him go crazy trying to find you—especially when he didn't believe that I didn't know where you were—well, that was like payback time!' In spite of his contrition, there was a gleam of remembered spite in the brown eyes. 'Then later, when that postcard you sent caught up with me, well, I guess I enjoyed the idea of secretly putting one over on him. And I could see you were so happy here, so I convinced myself that not saying anything was for the best...only that was self-serving, too, because of the money—'

'Oh, God, Karl, did he tell you about that?'' she choked out. 'How I *stole* from him?'

'No, you didn't—'

'I just found the case of money up in the cupboard.'

'It was me. *I* took it. You called me to come and see you that day. Flint was in Wellington for a two-day auction and you were upset, talking about how unhappy you were and how you wanted to get away somewhere and think for a few days. I told you I was going to Sydney on a selling trip that night and you said you'd come along, so I booked an extra ticket from your bedroom phone while you threw some things in a bag.

'You were so distracted you were packing all sorts of silly stuff and then, when you got a bundle of junk out of the safe with your passport, you just left it wide open. I saw the money there and thought serves the bastard right! So I shovelled the lot into one of your bags before I left. You were supposed to meet me later at the airport, but you never showed up and I just thought you'd calmed down and changed your mind...until Ryan rang my motel in Sydney wanting to know if I'd heard from you.'

Ryan was right. With no emotional awareness of what Karl was telling her, Nina felt she was hearing the plot of a soap opera—a particularly *bad* soap opera. She did, however, have a vivid memory of getting out of a taxi stopped at a red traffic light on downtown Auckland's waterfront road and being pursued by the angry driver for the fare as she walked towards the big sign for harbour ferries to Waiheke and Shearwater Islands.

As soon as she'd seen it, she'd known the sign was an omen. Sydney had suddenly seemed too far away. Everything had seemed remote except the certain knowledge that, if she could only get to Shearwater, see Puriri Bay again, then whatever was wrong with her life would be put right again.

'But the money... Why didn't you at least make sure it got back to him instead of letting him believe—'

'How could I, without implicating myself? And anyway, I couldn't because it wasn't all there,' he admitted sullenly, his words slightly muffled by the rag. 'Didn't you ever wonder where I got the backing to buy into this surf-wear thing?' He read the expression on her face and shrugged.

'Yeah, well, I suppose you would have thought that, but I'm out of the weed business for good. No, I nosed that money out the first time I came over here. I used to pick it up in instalments, like from my own private bank, whenever I came over to see you. I'm sorry, Nina. God! I know it seems I was just using this whole situation for my own ends, but there was a lot more to it than that. I really figured I owed it to you not to let you be found until you showed signs you *wanted* to be found.

'And I've totally cleaned up my act now. I'm not even drinking booze and I haven't touched any of that money for months. I've got a chance to make something of my life and I don't want to stuff it up by having this hanging over me. At least Flint knows now that it was me. And I've told him I can pay it back to him in instalments—I'm really working hard and sales are booming. Don't look like that. I'll pay him back—all of it—I promise.'

Nina had heard Karl's promises before. Maybe this time he *was* sincere, she thought wearily.

'You keep on saying you wanted to see me happy again.

But I don't understand. I know I loved him, Karl—I still do. So why was I so unhappy? Why couldn't I cope with our life together? What was it that I was running away from?'

Karl tried to check if he was still bleeding and winced as the rag stuck to his lip. 'I can't tell you that,' he grunted.

'Can't—or won't?' she asked grimly.

He was stiff with his unaccustomed restraint. 'I'm trying to do the right thing here, okay?' He had never been physically demonstrative, but now he gave her a quick hug, as if he was afraid a longer one would be rejected. 'He said he didn't want me to tell you…but I'm not going to tell you *anyway*.' His attempted humour at his own expense fell totally flat.

'Blame me all you like, but don't take it out on him. He's never let you down the way I have,' Karl said soberly. 'He told me I'd done enough damage and he's right, so I'm taking myself out of the frame—going right back on the next ferry.' He gave her a little push in the direction of the house. 'You wanted to go after him, so go. He's a proud man. He won't wait forever….'

CHAPTER NINE

'YOU can't mean to leave *now!*'

Nina watched in dismay as Ryan meticulously folded his few items of clothing and put them into his leather bag on top of the bundles of money that she had given him the previous day.

'I have a business to run,' he said, collecting his toiletries from the dresser. 'I've been away too long.'

She was bewildered by the excuse. Even though she had heard him discussing business on his cell phone several times over the past few days, he had never given any sign that he was impatient to return. One of the reasons that his string of individualistic galleries had been so highly successful was his ability to delegate: he hired the brightest talents in the business and trusted them to do their jobs.

'But you're supposed to still be on holiday—'

'Some holiday,' he said wryly, touching the contusion just above his eye that Nina spent ten minutes icing after she had rushed back to the house. Truth to tell, she had done it more for the chance to touch him and force him to listen to her than for reasons of first aid.

At least tending his facial bruises had given her a chance to explain face to face why she had appeared to be defending Karl. Ryan had seemed to believe her, his black mood slowly dissipating under her wifely fussing. But although she had told him what Karl had prompted her to remember about the day she had left him, he had resisted any in-depth conversation about the state of their marriage, and Nina had been too aware of the frightening fragility of their relationship to force the issue with an argument.

164

She had naively consoled herself with thought that they would have all the time in the world to discuss their future and their past...especially when he had later taken her to bed and made love to her with a tender savagery that made her heart soar with love.

'This island is proving rather hazardous to my health,' he continued ruefully. 'Perhaps it's your magical place trying to protect you from unwelcome intruders.'

'I'm sorry—' she began.

'I'm not,' he cut her off bluntly. 'This time it was purely my own fault. I hit him first. And I enjoyed it...especially since your interference meant I didn't get to land many more righteous punches.'

'It's kind of you to allow him time to pay the money.'

'Kindness has nothing to do with it. I'm giving him a loan on his investment—the longer he takes to pay, the more interest he owes me, so I can't lose.' He zipped up the bag and looked around the empty room. 'I have one or two more things to do for Ray and then I'll take the afternoon ferry.'

The same one on which he had arrived. In a week, life had gone full circle. But he was a man of his word, she told herself...whether it was a promise to an old man or a vow to his wife.

'Ray'll be sorry that you're going,' she said desperately. 'You know how much he enjoys your company.' *Please don't go.*

'Ray understands how it is,' he returned, shrugging, then carried the bag through to the living room and placed it by the couch.

But I don't! Nina wailed in her heart. How could he make love to her the way he had last night and then calmly walk out today as if it had just been a casual one-night stand?

'But we've barely had a chance to talk,' she said as he

laid his heavy coat over the back of a chair. 'When are you coming back?'

'I'm not.' The blow was all the more vicious for being totally unexpected. 'I've said all I have to say over the past week. It's your move now. As Karl so succinctly put it before I hit him, I can't force you to be someone you don't want to be. I can't make the decisions for both of us. You're the one to decide what your next step will be. I'm going to give you the space to do that. And meantime, I have a home, a life, waiting for me.'

'But…I'm your *wife*,' she reminded him in despair, spreading her hands in helpless appeal for his understanding.

He captured her left hand and turned it over, studying the simple gold band that was back on her finger, rubbing it slowly with his thumb. 'This isn't magical, you know. A ring doesn't make you a wife, Nina.'

'I know that.' Vows and a loving heart did. She pressed her other hand to her chest. 'But I *remember*…I *feel* that I'm your wife. That was what you wanted, wasn't it? What you came here for?'

His fingers tightened on hers, colour streaking along his lean cheekbones, his blue eyes flaring with hope. 'Are you saying you're ready to leave Puriri Bay with me…to come back home?'

Leave? *Now?* She hesitated. Too much had happened in too short a time. Unreasoning fear reared its ugly head. 'I—I still have a few paintings to do for George, but if you stayed, we could talk…' She saw the wall instantly go up behind his eyes and said wretchedly, 'You can't just *leave* like this, with nothing resolved—'

She broke off as his mouth twisted sardonically.

'Why not? *You* did. At least *you're* getting the courtesy of a goodbye.'

She gasped in pain at the slashing thrust.

'I'm sorry!' He was as swift to apologise as he had been to attack. It was his generosity of spirit that had helped turn the violent physical attraction that she had initially fought against feeling for him into something much richer, sweeter and far more enduring.

'I'm sorry,' Ryan said again, lifting her slender hand to his mouth, his lips warm as they pressed over her ring. 'That was below the belt. Forgive me. It was frustration talking. I know that it was your amnesia that stopped your getting in touch with me. I accept that all the doubts and suspicions I had about you over the past nine months were wrong, that you wouldn't knowingly have wanted to hurt me as you did.'

She cupped his cheek with her other hand. 'And you *were* hurt, weren't you?' she ventured, probing the wound that still festered between them.

The desolation in his eyes tore at her bruised heart, but there was strength and determination in his tone. 'I didn't marry you because I had to, Nina, but because I *wanted* to. We were lovers in every sense of the word, both before and after the wedding. You're the only woman I've ever wanted as my wife.'

Was he using the past tense? Nina looked desperately into his eyes. 'Why are you doing this to me?' she whispered. 'You crash back into my life and then just when I'm coming to terms with it, you go away again. Is it to pay me back for what I did?'

'No...God, no.' He led her to the couch and sat her down, playing gravely with her fingers as he said, 'But, Nina, at the time I married you, you were very vulnerable. It wasn't that long since your grandmother had died. You thought you'd been fully prepared for her death because you had anticipated it for so long, but afterwards it hit you a lot harder than you expected. I'm seven years older than you and decades more experienced. I decided I wanted you and deliberately plotted to sweep you off your feet.'

She nodded, her eyes misty, remembering being whisked into a world of wonder, showered by his passionate attentions. A world where she was wined, dined, flattered and seduced by his dynamic personality and fiery devotion to her sexual pleasure. Her initial insecurity—her doubts that she was just a sexual challenge to him or that she was allowing herself to be overwhelmed by his wealth—was swiftly overridden by the strength of her feelings.

'I arrogantly assumed that I alone had the power to make you completely happy. And then, when I came here, I continued to arrogantly assume that I knew you better than you knew yourself.' His glance encompassed the cosy room. 'But having seen your work...the way you're painting...I can see that you've fulfilled yourself here in a way that you never managed to do during our time together, even with all the material advantages I could provide. I have to admire and respect what you've done. Maybe you're right after all, about this being where you really belong. Maybe this is the price I have to pay for my foolish arrogance—freeing you to decide *my* happiness.'

She felt his hope like a brand on her heart. 'You don't have to do it this way.'

His eyes were implacably steady as he stood up, drawing her to her feet. 'I do, and one day I hope you'll understand why.' He felt in his pocket. 'Here, I want you to have this.' Something smooth and heavy slipped into her palm. His silver cigarette lighter.

'A souvenir of your flying visit?' She splashed him with the acid of her disappointment.

His bruised face welcomed the evidence of her fighting spirit. 'No, hopefully something to remind you of what you're missing.'

As if she would need any reminding! She looked down.

Each moment she spent with him, some blurred detail from those two years slipped into sharper focus.

'I gave this to you,' she said, recalling, her voice softening as she re-read the engraving. No wonder the weight of it had felt familiar the night he had washed up in the storm. 'You admired it at a jewellery exhibition, but you said it was ridiculous to own a cigarette lighter when you'd given up smoking in your teens. But I could see that you loved it, so I bought it for your birthday.' The money hadn't been what attracted her to him, but there were certain undeniable advantages to being the wife of a rich man!

'Along with an exquisite candelabra so I'd have plenty of cause to use it with a socially acceptable flourish,' he finished with a deep chuckle.

Her fingers uncurled reluctantly. 'I can't take this.'

'The giver was always more important to me than the gift. They're a matched set as far as I'm concerned,' he said softly, 'that I hope will soon be restored to me intact. You never did explain to me what the words you had engraved meant,' he added. 'I guessed they were a quote of some kind, but I could never track down the reference— it's certainly not from Shakespeare.'

She had teased and tantalised him with her secret knowledge, knowing that he delighted in the challenge, knowing that one day, when the time was ripe, she would tell him what she had then been too insecure to put into words, halfappalled by the intensity of her own feelings.

Now was her chance. Nina threw back her head proudly and looked at him with clear green eyes. 'It's Ralph Waldo Emerson. "Love is the bright foreigner, the foreign self." It means that you're my love—the foreign part of myself. An indivisible part.'

Her bold gamble paid off, but only briefly. His face tautened with a triumphant, predatory hunger. His hands reached for her, then just before contact, clenched into furious fists of self-denial that he forced back down to his sides.

'Ah, the same man who said that "Art is a jealous mistress",' he quoted shakily, his voice growing progressively steadier with each word as he mastered his emotions. 'No wonder you thought he was an appropriate source of wisdom.'

That's all he had to say! She makes a passionate declaration of love and he flips a breezy quote back at her?

'Ryan—'

'Don't, Nina,' he cautioned her roughly. 'This isn't only a matter of whether we love each other. Sometimes love just isn't enough.' He turned aside from her frown. 'Talking of art—I do want something from you in exchange for borrowing my lighter.'

Borrowing? She liked the confident use of that word. 'Oh?' Her spirits lifted.

'Some of your paintings,' he said, smoothly assuming the protective cloak of his professional demeanour. 'I meant what I said about admiring them. I'd like to take a few back for the gallery and see how they go. We'll sell them on commission, of course. I'll get my secretary to send you our standard contract, and if you have anything you want to renegotiate, you can call me. Oh, and tell George to get in touch with me if he's serious about doing that launch.'

For 'contract' she heard 'contact', and everything else faded out as her panicked sense of urgency relaxed. Ryan wasn't cutting himself out from her life; he wasn't going back to the mainland in order to forget everything that had happened in the past week. He was making sure she knew that their lives would remain entwined even if only professionally....

They sorted out four paintings, which Nina carefully wrapped with paper and string, then he took his bag over with him to Ray's. 'He said Chas Peterson will run me over to the ferry in his car. No sense in us enduring a long public goodbye.'

Nina could see wonderful sense! 'I thought I'd come down to the wharf with you.'

He shook his head. 'I'd rather you didn't. I don't want to see you standing on that jetty getting smaller and smaller until you wink out of my sight. It's a kind of private nightmare of mine I'd rather not have visited on me during my waking hours.'

She granted him his fears, but on the eve of his departure he couldn't stop her flinging herself into his arms for a desperate, yearning kiss as Ray and Chas discreetly turned their attention to loading the boot of the car.

'Ryan...?' She slid an uneasy mental tendril out to the wall, testing it for flaws. 'If I do come back...it's something truly awful, isn't it?' she whispered, touching his face. 'Something happened that's too horrible for you to talk about.'

His eyes had that bleak, haunted look that made her unravel inside, and he stole the remains of her breath in a fierce hug that squeezed tears from her eyes.

She opened her mouth to tell him that she had changed her mind, that she would come, but she couldn't force the words out past the paralysing fear, and the helpless tears seeped into the corners of her mouth.

'For better or for worse, Nina. Sometimes they're impossibly mixed up, for you don't know which is which. But whenever you're ready for the worst, you know where to find me,' he said raggedly. He bent to pick up Zorro and rub his jaw against the animal's furry ears. 'And take care of this little guy for me.'

He handed the dog to Nina as if he knew she needed something warm and alive to fill her empty arms. Her eyes widened as she accepted the gentle transfer of weight, felt the sensation of a small heart beating rapidly against hers.

When Ryan turned his back to shake hands with Ray, Zorro seemed to sense that something was dreadfully wrong and began to whine and squirm in her arms, and once the car had disappeared from sight, he proved inconsolable, not even showing any interest in a thrown stick.

'I'll take him home with me and see if a bone will cheer him up,' Nina told Ray in a thickened voice.

'Take more than a bone if you ask me,' Ray told her, leaning heavily on his cane. 'You think a nice meal is going to be enough to make you perky?'

The very thought of food made her want to vomit, but it hadn't been an invitation.

'Why don't you go after him, Nina?' he urged. 'The ferry's not due to leave for another twenty minutes. You could still make it if you took the short cut over the track.'

Nina shook her head, wiping the dampness from her cheeks. 'I need time to think.'

'What's to think about? A wife's place is with her husband.'

For better or for worse.

The strain of the day made her temper snap. 'These are liberated times, Ray. Sometimes it's the husband's place to be with his wife!'

'Well, I hope that liberated thought keeps you warm these cold nights. Here, give Zorro to me. He's not going to cheer up with you drooping around him like a wet week!'

She didn't have the heart to argue, and back in her lonely house, instead of turning to the botanical work she had claimed that she had to do, she sat at the table, sipping hot, sweet coffee just the way Ryan always liked it, leafing through the wedding photos that she had found in the dusty satchel.

They were informal, not the self-consciously posed, air-brushed results of a conventional wedding photographer, but the casual artistry of one of Ryan's friends, who regularly exhibited his off-beat photographic portraits at the Pacific Rim. He had captured, not just images on paper, but emotions, too.

It had been a gloriously hot day, but windy, and one of the photos showed Nina giggling outside the church as she tried to stop the little fly-away veil on her hat from literally flying away, and Ryan looked particularly devilish in another as he failed to prevent her gauzy cream skirts billowing up to flash her suspender-clad thighs at the blushing vicar.

It had been barely three years ago, and while Nina had been plumper, it was Ryan who had changed more. In one shot, taken across the top of the black Rolls-Royce, the two of them were caught in quiet discussion, and although Ryan's face was unsmiling, it was also totally unguarded. There were no tiny lines of tension around his eyes, no controlled pull at the corners of his mouth, no shadows in the intent eyes.

In spite of his gravity, he looked carefree, contented, younger than his thirty years. It was the trusting face of a man who had put his faith in the future and was eager for anything it might bring. Ryan wasn't fearless—he wasn't that stupid—but he had always had the courage to admit his fears because, as he pointed out, it was difficult to fight an enemy you couldn't see.

That's what Nina was trying to do. She was fighting blind against an enemy that she refused to acknowledge even existed. It was a battle she could never win because in the end she was only fighting herself. The result must be an endless stalemate.

She looked at the ring on her finger, the symbol of love and fidelity. Of trust. Ryan had said that sometimes love wasn't enough. But sometimes it was.

Sometimes all it took was a willingness to put your faith in that love.

Three days later, Nina was miserably clutching the rail

of the Auckland-bound ferry as it dipped and rolled on a sullenly unpleasant sea. She didn't know whether it was the toasted cheese she had had for breakfast, the ghastly apprehension that knotted her stomach or just a simple case of seasickness that was making her feel so queasy. She didn't care; all she wanted to do was get off the boat!

She would have been travelling three days ago, when the sea had still been calm, if she had obeyed her first impulse. But Ray had persuaded her that, since she had missed her chance to catch Ryan before he left, she might as well take the time to do the whole thing right and proper.

So while the weather was blowing up, she had tied up all her flapping loose ends, closed up her house, packed her belongings, and here she was heading for a surprise visit to her husband. She hadn't dared let him know that she was on her way. What if she lost her nerve and couldn't make it? What if she couldn't force herself to get off the boat once it docked in Auckland? Although the way she was currently feeling, she intended to be first onto dry land!

As the ferry chugged into calmer waters approaching the wharves that fringed the downtown area, Nina shakily stepped back from the rail and sat on the wooden bench running along the outside wall of the cabin. She fumbled in her shoulder-bag and drew out the photographs that had become her talisman.

She drew her thumb across the glossy surface, down the flighty flounces of the multilayered, silk chiffon dress. Her head was resting against Ryan's shoulder as they both looked at the camera, the rest of her in profile, the wind pressing the thin, cream silk panels lovingly to her body below Ryan's linking hands under her breasts and revealing an extra curvaceousness that only an artist's finely discerning eye might notice.

A jolt ripped up Nina's spine.

I didn't marry you because I had to, but because I wanted to.

Her eyes narrowed on the photograph, fiercely blinked away the annoying fuzziness that was trying to encroach on her vision. Her face was a little fuller than it was now, and her breasts rounder...her belly...

I didn't marry you because I had to...

She closed her eyes, her hand creeping to her rocky stomach. Her rocky, *flat* stomach. Though her hips were wider than she would have liked, she could never remember carrying any extra padding around the front of her tummy.

Except...

Oh, God...oh, God...oh, God...

Her consciousness blinked on and off in time to the chant, a kaleidoscope of confusing images tumbling through her head.

Oh, God...oh, God...oh, God...

More images began to take shape, past blending with present until she didn't know which was which.

Ryan's finger tracing the thready silver lines on her skin after they'd made love...

Ryan massaging her swollen belly.

Ryan handing her Zorro—a tiny, warm, living bundle to cradle against her breast...

No, not Zorro...

Oh, no...oh, no...oh, no...

A sharp agony lanced her skull and the light snapped off inside her mind, abruptly shutting down the flow of mental images. Her eyes flew open, and she looked down again at the subtly damning photo.

This time, her conscious intelligence subverted her subconscious attempt to manipulate the evidence of her eyes.

That fashionable, multilayered look had hidden a multitude of sins. Specifically hers and Ryan's.

The bride had been pregnant!

Still in the first trimester, but far enough along to show a body ripening into motherhood, and a special glow to her eyes and skin that had nothing to do with the excitement of the day.

Ryan had only asked her to marry him after she had told him that she was pregnant.

If it hadn't been for the baby, he mightn't have even married her at all.

The baby...

Nina put the photographs away and clenched her hands in her lap, deliberately censoring her thoughts. She couldn't go back now. The wall had collapsed with a vengeance. Pandora's box was wide open, and not all the will in the world was going to put the evil safely back inside. With the traumatic return of her memory, all her other memories had returned. Now the most she could do was try to keep the pain at a manageable level until she reached her destination. It was more important now than ever that she not flinch from the task ahead: her journey home.

But, unlike before, this time her repression of harrowing memories took a concentrated effort that exhausted her store of strength. So when it came time to get off the ferry, Nina just allowed herself to be carried along with the rest of the morning commuters, ignoring the cheery apology of the crewman by the gangplank that it must be the fault of the following wind and the captain's desire to outrun the rain squalls that they were ten minutes earlier than the scheduled time of arrival.

It had been so long since she'd been in the city that she was immediately assailed on all sides by the sounds, sights and smells of teeming humanity. The wind blowing in off the harbour was almost rain and a light dusting of moisture pearled on Nina's green woollen sweater and soaked into her slim-fitting black pants. It was rush hour and consequently taxis were in short supply, so Nina struggled across the road and up the block in order to lurk under the canopy of an up-market hotel and snaffle one as it disgorged a passenger, doing it right under the nose of the supercilious doorman.

Each tick of the meter that brought her nearer her goal made her heart beat faster until she was afraid it was going to leap out of her chest. She wanted to scream at the driver to go faster at the same time as she longed to beg him to slow down. When the taxi finally turned into the long, sweeping, tree-lined driveway of the sprawling white house, Nina was almost faint with apprehension, stepping out on jellied legs as the driver unloaded her bags and, seeing how pale she was looking, actually condescended to carry them up the white marble steps and set them down by the imposing front door.

'You okay, luv?' he asked as she counted out the dollars with shaking hands. 'Looking pretty peaky—not pregnant, are you?' he added with the cheerful insensitivity of a man who made his living chatting to strangers.

'No.'

Nina didn't think it was possible that she could feel any fainter than she already did, but suddenly she did.

Oh, God, how did she know that she *wasn't* pregnant? If Ryan had been carrying any condoms with him, he certainly hadn't produced them, and she had been so deep in her state of denial she hadn't even thought about birth control when they were making love.

She had acted as if sex had no connection with procreation because to connect babies and Ryan in her mind was simply too agonising. The last time she had fallen pregnant it had been the result of that single first volcanic encounter—after which Ryan had always used protection. What chance had such a fertile couple of avoiding conception when they had made love *dozens* of times on Shearwater without any attempt at prevention?

Oh, God, she couldn't bear to go through all that again....

As the taxi drove off, Nina fumbled for her key. Ryan had told her that, contrary to commonsense, he hadn't changed the locks after she left. He had continued to hope that one day he would come home and find her there, waiting for him. Now she knew why. His rage over her betrayal had always been undermined by his compassion.

The large, black-and-white-tiled foyer was empty and Nina drifted like a ghost through the beautifully furnished rooms. Everything was the same as she remembered. Even the fresh-cut flowers in the tall vases were blossoms she recognised from her plantings in the huge garden. Tears stung her eyes. She was home. Nothing had changed.

Everything had changed.

She put her foot on the first step of the sweeping staircase and looked up. A stairway to heaven, she had laughed wickedly the first time Ryan had swept her up to his bedroom.

Now it was a stairway she must climb to face her private hell.

The marble stair rail was cool under her fingertips as she rounded the curve. She was vaguely aware of noises outside and the slamming of doors and voices, but she kept steadily climbing. She was already on the top step when she heard rapid footsteps striding across the ceramic tiles below.

'Teresa, did you see her come in? Her bags are outside. Nina? *Nina?*' The deep, masculine voice lifted an octave at the precise moment he saw her, expressing a soaring relief. *'Nina!'* This was followed by a tense exclamation of sharpening alarm. 'Nina? Where are you going?'

She kept moving along the thick cream carpet of the wide hallway. Behind her, she could hear the slap of shoes on the marble stairs, punctuated by grunted breaths as Ryan bounded up them two and three at a time.

'Nina—wait!'

The doors to most of the rooms off the hallway were ajar, but the fourth one on the left was closed and Nina reached for the white ceramic doorhandle.

A swarthy masculine hand got there first and held the door shut. 'Nina? What are you doing?' She looked at him, and he drew a sharp breath at the grim set of her pale face. 'Ray rang and told me you'd got on the ferry. I went to pick you up from the terminal, but I got held up by a damned traffic accident and must have missed you.' He was talking quickly to distract her, but his blue eyes were slowly inspecting her, eating her up with his concern.

She cleared her tight throat. 'Open the door.'

His hand tightened defensively, the knuckles flaring white. He was wearing his wedding ring again, she noticed, a shaft of warm light melting the black chill in her heart. 'I wanted to be here with you when you arrived. I've asked Teresa to make us some coffee. If you come back downstairs, we can—'

'Open the door.'

His rangy body tensed, his lean face contracting with fear. 'Nina, you've only just got here. Give yourself time to adjust. You don't have to do this right now—'

'I've had all the time I can bear...' Her voice broke and she tried again. 'I remember...I remembered while I was coming over on the ferry. You don't have to protect me any more, Ryan. I'm tired of being afraid.' She put her hand over his and applied pressure that was part plea, part command. 'Just open the door.'

He held her gaze for a long moment, then said quietly, 'All right...but together. We face everything together. And I'll never stop wanting to protect you.'

They slowly pushed the door open and entered the room. A room painted eggshell-blue with white trim, and a motif of teddy bears stencilled around the bottom of the walls.

Stuffed animals and toys sat along the top of a white book-case crammed with children's books and a large teddy bear sat on a white cane chair.

Nina moved slowly around the room, picking up and putting down items, including the teddy bear, which she raised to her face, breathing in faint hints of baby powder. Ryan hovered quietly at her side, his jaw clenched as he watched her pale expression become brittle with grief.

An empty blue cot stood along one wall and over it a mobile of coloured aeroplanes gently rocked in acknowledgment of their presence. Next to the cot, a dresser displayed blue-framed photographs: of Nina and of Ryan, and of the little boy with the curly black hair and blue eyes astride his push-along horse. The photograph she hadn't wanted to see. Nina picked it up.

'Liam…' The name was a sigh on her lips and an ache in her heart. 'Liam…'

Her son. So bright and full of promise. Her bundle of joy, snatched away so violently, his merry spirits quenched in an instant.

She put the photograph down and touched the upper rail of the cot. 'We were going to move this out and get him a proper bed because he'd started learning to climb out,' she said softly. 'He took his first steps the week before he died. My baby was growing up so fast….'

Ryan moved in behind her, his hands settling on her shoulders. 'Nina…'

She wrenched away from his touch and spun around. 'He was only one year old—he didn't deserve to die!'

Ryan's face filled with a torment to match her own. 'No, no, he didn't. And if I hadn't suggested we go down to the marina that day—'

'No!' Nina flung herself back at him, surrounding him with her arms. 'God, no—it wasn't your fault. It was a freak accident. I *never* blamed you.'

The aluminium-alloy dive tank that had exploded, killing Liam and the marina employee who had just refilled it and injuring several others, had been found to be faulty. But no amount of hindsight or offer of compensation could make up to Nina for the loss of her son.

'I *never* blamed you,' she repeated savagely. 'You were hurt, too. I thought I had lost you, as well.' Tears began pouring down her face. 'I couldn't bear it—I...I couldn't have borne to lose you *both*....' And suddenly, she was sobbing violently against his chest, hoarse, gut-wrenching sobs that shook both their bodies.

'Oh, Nina, thank God,' Ryan murmured in anguished relief as he buried his face in her hair and rocked her from side to side, allowing her the luxury of her long-delayed grief. 'Thank God you're back, and safe, and able to cry for our lovely little boy and cherish him in your memory again. You never cried for him after the funeral. You held everything tightly inside you. You tried to be so brave, to pretend for my sake that you were all right, that you were coping better day by day so I wouldn't worry about you. I tried to believe that, but you *weren't* all right. Months crept past and you still weren't eating or sleeping properly, you couldn't paint, you didn't want to talk about Liam except in the most superficial way, you never set foot in this room. I think the accident must have brought your memories of your mother's death too close to the surface, so you tried to repress them both, and the pressure inside you built up until you just couldn't take it any more.'

'So I ran away. In my mind I ran away...and I left you to face this all alone. I'm so sorry,' she sobbed. 'I'm so *sorry*. Please don't hate me.'

'How can I hate my foreign self? Nina, twice in your life you've witnessed the death of people you loved in explosions. How could you *not* find that unbearably traumatising? You were in deep shock yourself, yet you cradled

Liam's body until the ambulance came and still had the presence of mind to put my belt around my leg as a tourniquet. You saved my leg if not my *life*. I may have been angry and hurt, and frustrated by you, but I never, ever stopped loving you.'

'He looked so whole and perfect, I couldn't believe he was gone,' she whispered against his shuddering heart. 'There wasn't even any blood.'

'It was the concussive shock to the brain that killed him. He wasn't hit with shrapnel like me. It was a blessing of a kind, darling, being so instant. He didn't have time to suffer.'

'Like we have.' She lifted her head and saw that his olive cheeks, too, were tracked with the glittering evidence of his solitary grief, now shared. 'I thought...I was afraid...that with Liam gone... He *was* the reason that you asked me to marry you when you did.'

His arms tightened across her back. 'Foolish woman,' he chided fiercely. 'Your getting pregnant changed only the timing of my proposal. I'd already been rehearsing one for weeks, trying to think of a way to phrase it so that you wouldn't reject me for trying to rush you into something you weren't ready for. I knew that sometimes your cautious soul worried everything was happening too fast.'

'So...you weren't sorry?'

'Sorry? I was glad. I *loved* the idea of your having my baby. I loved seeing your pregnancy grow and I loved Liam. Even though we had him for such a short time, and through all the pain and grief, I never regretted for one moment that we had had him to add to the sum of our love.'

That brought on another tormenting doubt. 'I just don't know if... I know how much you want a family, but I don't know if I can ever risk having another baby—going through that kind of loss again,' she blurted.

He cupped her face and kissed the agony from her brow. 'We have each other. That's what matters most to me. The giver, not the gift, remember?'

They lingered a little longer amongst the poignant memories of their beloved son and then Ryan led Nina by the hand to the master bedroom next door where the wardrobes were still divided into his and hers, crammed with all the clothes she had left behind.

'To have and to hold, Nina,' Ryan said thickly as they lay down on the wide bed and cuddled together in sweet, passionless intimacy, talking in low voices, reminiscing, crying, laughing. When Ryan finally glanced at his watch, he was startled to see how the time had slipped away.

'Teresa will have made and dumped out umpteen cups of coffee by now,' he said, urging Nina up. 'And I have something to show you.' He looked briefly uncertain. 'That's if... I assume by the number of bags that you're not just here for the weekend?'

'I've closed up the cottage,' she said huskily. 'George is extremely miffed with me, but Ray was all for it. He said he could manage quite well on his own.' She had been a little hurt by the cavalier way the old man had treated her departure.

Ryan chuckled. 'That's because with what he's stinging me on the sale, he can afford to employ a full-time housekeeper to boss around for the rest of his life.'

'You're *buying* the house in Puriri Bay?' Nina was stunned.

'Actually, *you're* buying it. I was planning to put the deed in your name. I want you to know that your magical isle is there whenever you need it.'

Nina felt a flash of fear. 'You think this might happen to me again?'

He took her hands in a reassuring grip. 'No. From what I've read—and Dave Freeman has told me—dissociative amnesia is rarely repeated. It's an isolated episode, like an accident, complete in itself.'

'I'm going to see a doctor,' she announced as they went back down the stairs. 'Just to make sure.'

'If that's what you want—' Ryan broke off at the sound of a high-pitched squeaking, and suddenly a diminutive, long-haired Jack Russell puppy came slipping and sliding out the door to the kitchen across the black-and-white tiles, a black sock dangling from its mouth.

'Come back here, you little bandit!' Teresa Robson's large bulk bobbed into sight as Nina captured the furry fugitive and lifted him up gently in her cupped hands. 'Oh, so you found her, then, Mr Flint. Lovely to have you back again, Mrs Flint! And aren't you looking a picture!' she said, beaming, as if Nina had just arrived back from a successful weekend shopping trip.

Nina, aware of her blotchy, tear-swollen face, pillow-ruffled hair and crumpled clothes, smiled ruefully back. 'Nice to see you, too, Teresa. And who's this?' Her gaze moved from the tiny puppy in her hands, who was trying to lick her salty chin, to Ryan's sheepish face.

'Ah…I only bought him yesterday. He hasn't got a name yet,' he admitted. 'I thought you might like to think of one,' he said, and her heart melted a little more.

'How about Bandit?' she suggested, gently removing the sock and handing it to the housekeeper, slipping easily back into the old routine. 'Could we have that coffee Ryan asked for in the lounge, Teresa, if it hasn't gone cold?'

'I'll have it there in a tick…and some scones I've just whipped up. And let me take the little one back. I think he's overdue for a purposeful visit to the garden!'

'Is that what you wanted to show me?' Nina asked Ryan as the incongruous pair vanished back into the kitchen.

'Well, *one* of the things,' he said mysteriously, and led

her out past the pool and up the wrought-iron staircase to her studio.

'*What on earth…?*' She walked into the formerly bland room and stared around her in amazement at the drop cloths and pencil drafting on all four walls and ceiling. Billowing clouds were waiting to be filled in on the graduated wash of blue sky that was beginning to stretch over the upper walls and ceiling. On the lower half of the walls, painting had only just begun on a small patch of the stunningly realistic, wind-ruffled sea.

'I thought…since you found it so inspirational to be painting on an island…that, well, you might like to feel that your studio was your private island, too. Not as magical, perhaps, but still a place for your creative imagination to soar free,' Ryan explained with endearing diffidence. 'Of course, if you don't like it, we can easily have it painted over again,' he added hastily.

Nina was revolving slowly and now she stopped, facing him, her eyes misting again, but this time with serene faith in her future with this wonderfully thoughtful, insightful man.

'I don't like it—I love it,' she said softly. 'But that's because of the giver, darling, not the gift.' And she felt in her pocket for his silver lighter and handed it to him as she had handed him her heart: his cherished matched set.

CHAPTER TEN

NINA placed the sheaf of flowers on the bright square of neatly clipped grass and rose to her feet, her eyes lingering on the gold letters etched into the polished granite slab.

Liam Robert Flint
Aged 12 months
Beloved son

She smiled sadly. He would have been ten years old today. She turned and walked through the sleepy cemetery next to the small wooden church in which she and Ryan had been married.

As she opened the low gate in the old-fashioned white picket fence, she saw an overweight Jack Russell terrier come scooting around from the back of the church, hotly pursued by a laughing boy and girl, a tall man jogging with loose-limbed grace up the rear.

'Daddy says we can sail to the island tomorrow and stay for the whole weekend at the bach! And Grampa Ray is going to tell me how to catch a big, man-eating shark!' shouted the smaller of the two children, a dainty, mop-topped little girl in a frilly pink dress and grass-stained white shoes. She skipped to a screeching halt, almost tripping over the wheezing dog, who had dropped the slobbery stick he was carrying at Nina's feet.

'Is he, darling?' Nina said, straightening her daughter's hopelessly twisted dress, now covered with biddy-bids. 'And what are you going to do, Tony?'

The skinny, dark-haired six-year-old looked up at her

with shiny green eyes, his sturdy chin jutting. 'I'm going to paint a whale for Daddy's office,' he said with the dignity of one who had several works pinned up in that august establishment. Dignity was soon forgotten in the desire to score over a mere five-year-old. 'A whale is way bigger than a shark, you know, Sara.'

The little girl poked her tongue out at him in answer.

'It took me a while to find them,' their father said, his blue eyes warm with love as they studied Nina's tranquil face, his blue-black hair—now liberally flecked with what he liked to call distinguished grey—tousled by his run. 'The vicar had them pulling weeds in his garden—or in Bandit's case, digging a hole to China!'

'What do you and Daddy like doing best on Shearwater Island, Mummy?' Sara asked curiously.

Nina caught the wicked gleam in Ryan's eyes as they glanced at each other over the top of Sara's innocent head, and they both burst out laughing.

And despite their children's gleeful pestering, refused to explain what was so funny.

*An electric chemistry with a disturbingly
familiar stranger...
A reawakening of passions long forgotten...
And a compulsive desire to get to know
this stranger all over again!*

Because

**What the memory has lost,
the body never forgets**

In Harlequin Presents®
over the coming months look out for:

BACK IN THE MARRIAGE BED
by Penny Jordan
On sale September, #2129

SECRET SEDUCTION
by Susan Napier
On sale October, #2135

THE SICILIAN'S MISTRESS
by Lynne Graham
On sale November, #2139

Available wherever Harlequin books are sold.

If you enjoyed what you just read,
then we've got an offer you can't resist!

Take 2 bestselling love stories FREE!
Plus get a FREE surprise gift!

You're not going to believe this offer!

In October and November 2000, buy any two Harlequin
or Silhouette books and save $10.00 off future purchases,
or buy any three and save $20.00 off future purchases!

Just fill out this form and attach 2 proofs of purchase (cash register
receipts) from October and November 2000 books and Harlequin will
send you a coupon booklet worth a total savings of $10.00 off future
purchases of Harlequin and Silhouette books in 2001. Send us 3 proofs
of purchase and we will send you a coupon booklet worth a total
savings of $20.00 off future purchases.

Saving money has never been this easy.

I accept your offer! Please send me a coupon booklet:

Name: _____

Address: _____ City: _____

State/Prov.: _____ Zip/Postal Code: _____

Optional Survey!

In a typical month, how many Harlequin or Silhouette books would you buy <u>new</u> at retail stores?

☐ Less than 1 ☐ 1 ☐ 2 ☐ 3 to 4 ☐ 5+

Which of the following statements best describes how you <u>buy</u> Harlequin or Silhouette books?
Choose one answer only that <u>best</u> describes you.

☐ I am a regular buyer and reader

☐ I am a regular reader but buy only occasionally

☐ I only buy and read for specific times of the year, e.g. vacations

☐ I subscribe through Reader Service but also buy at retail stores

☐ I mainly borrow and buy only occasionally

☐ I am an occasional buyer and reader

Which of the following statements best describes how you <u>choose</u> the Harlequin and Silhouette
series books you buy <u>new</u> at retail stores? By "series," we mean books within a particular line,
such as *Harlequin PRESENTS* or *Silhouette SPECIAL EDITION*. Choose one answer only that
<u>best</u> describes you.

☐ I only buy books from my favorite series

☐ I generally buy books from my favorite series but also buy
books from other series on occasion

☐ I buy some books from my favorite series but also buy from
many other series regularly

☐ I buy all types of books depending on my mood and what
I find interesting and have no favorite series

Please send this form, along with your cash register receipts as proofs of purchase, to:
In the U.S.: Harlequin Books, P.O. Box 9057, Buffalo, NY 14269
In Canada: Harlequin Books, P.O. Box 622, Fort Erie, Ontario L2A 5X3
(Allow 4-6 weeks for delivery) Offer expires December 31, 2000.   PHQ4002